Lions

Daredevils or Scaredycats

"Look, Mush. If I say you've got my place, you've got my place. Now get out of my place, Mush."

"No," said David Clifford.

"No?" echoed Fatty.

He couldn't believe his ears. Neither could we. We all gaped at the pair of them but mostly at David Clifford. He'd blushed to the roots of his pimples and was blinking furiously. Otherwise he looked quite sane. When Fatty spoke again it was with spine-chilling calm.

"Mush," he said. "I can have anything I want. Anything at all."

Chris Powling

Daredevils or Scaredycats

Lions
An Imprint of HarperCollins*Publishers*

First published in 1979 by Abelard Schuman Ltd
Published in Lions 1981
This edition published 1992

Lions is an imprint of HarperCollins Children's Books, a
division of HarperCollins Publishers Ltd, 77-85 Fulham Palace
Road, Hammersmith London W6 8JB

Printed and bound in Great Britain by HarperCollins Book
Manurfacturing Ltd, Glasgow

· The Crimson Pirate ·

If I'd been asked to draw David Clifford I'd
have started with his knees or his elbows or
his Adam's apple. He was that bony. None of
his clothes fitted him. This was because his
Mum bought them extra-large so he'd grow
into them but somehow he always grew in the
wrong direction. David Clifford had flat brown
hair that spilled over his eyes—or over his glasses
rather—and he was spotty and he collected train
numbers. Worst of all, he wore his school cap
wherever he went. Considering what a weed
David Clifford was, my brother Pete and I liked
him very much.

In fact there were only two things I didn't
like about David Clifford. The first was when
he beat me in the arithmetic test which most
weeks he did. The second was that he always
kept people waiting. He was keeping us waiting
right now.

"Won't be a minute," he'd said. "I'm just
finishing my egg."

He'd already been three minutes.

"Must be a blinkin' ostrich egg," I said bitterly. "How many do you think are in the queue now?"

"About four thousand."

"No, really."

"How should I know?" said Pete. I got up and went to the window. It had stopped snowing.

"That might keep a few kids away," I said hopefully.

"What might?"

"The snow. Plenty of kids'll prefer that to Saturday-morning Pictures."

"Not when it's *The Crimson Pirate*," Pete said. He was right. We'd been looking forward to *The Crimson Pirate* for weeks. So had most of the kids we knew. Some of them would have been queuing before eight o'clock. If you got there by half past eight, though, you ought to be all right ... I hoped. They did let in two hundred after all.

"Tell you somebody who will get in," said Pete, "queue or no queue."

"Who's that?" I asked as if I didn't know.

"Fatty Rosewell."

I laughed hollowly.

"Wouldn't it be funny if Fatty Rosewell were to come face to face with David Clifford!"

"It wouldn't," said Pete. "We'll be *with* David Clifford. So Fatty Rosewell would be coming face to face with us, too."

I hadn't thought of that. It wouldn't be at all funny. Being picked on by Fatty Rosewell was a weekly risk at Saturday-morning Pictures. So far we'd been lucky. It had always been someone else who'd copped it.

"Somehow I don't think David Clifford would be much use in a Rosewell bashing-up," I said nervously.

"Not much," Pete agreed. "Fatty could smash him to bits with his little finger. He'd end up in hospital. Still, that wouldn't be too bad for you."

"How come?"

"You'd come top in the arithmetic test for once." There were times when I'd have been quite happy to smash my twin brother to bits with my little finger. Before I could try, though, David Clifford came in.

"Ready?" he asked.

"Never been anything else," I snapped. "Let's get a move on."

On the way to the Odeon we hardly noticed the snow though it was the first that winter. Once or twice Pete picked up a handful and lobbed it at us, but I was too busy to retaliate. I was explaining to David Clifford how important it was to be in the first two hundred in the queue.

"I know," said David Clifford, "you told me."

"If we're even two hundred and one, two hundred and two and two hundred and three, we've had it. We've got to be there by about eight-thirty. The queue will have filled up by then."

"So you said."

"Supposing we're a hundred and ninety-nine, two hundred and two hundred and one?" asked my brother.

"One of us will have to drop out," I said.

"Yes, but which one?"

"We'd have to toss for it. Odd man out," David Clifford suggested.

I felt as if I'd swallowed a snowball. I started walking even faster, slithering a bit on the icy pavement.

"Hey, careful," said Pete. "We'll break our necks before we get there."

I'd have preferred that to losing the toss.

Halfway down College Slip we met Teddy and Jimmy. They were pulling a toboggan.

"My Dad made it," Jimmy said. "Coming down Martin's Hill?"

"No thanks," I said.

"This afternoon, maybe," said Pete.

"Snow'll be rotten by then," Teddy said. "Where you going?"

"Crimson Pirate."

"Think you'll get in?"

"Should do."

"See you then. Watch out for Fatty Rosewell!" We laughed.

"Who's Fatty Rosewell?" David Clifford asked. But by then we were on our way again. Teddy and Jimmy watched us go. They knew they'd made the wrong choice in preferring the snow, it seemed to me.

On the other hand maybe we had. It was only twenty past eight by the Odeon clock but already a crocodile of kids stretched from the

10

front steps round into the side alley. Old Grumpy, the commissionaire, was telling off the ones at the front.

"Twenty-five minutes before you go in," he was snarling, "another twenty-five minutes. So it's no good pushing and shoving."

"We'd better count," I said gloomily. "It might not be worth waiting."

"You count," said my brother to David Clifford. "You're good at arithmetic. Plenty of kids are jealous of your arithmetic and how you always come top in the test."

David Clifford beamed and began to count. For a while I tried to kick my brother, but the ground was too slippery and he was expecting it.

We moved along the queue. Counting wasn't easy. All of a sudden a group of kids would surge forward in a rush then protest loudly to Grumpy that it was the people behind stampeding *them* so he'd moan at the wrong lot. And the snowballs didn't help. Every so often these would explode off someone. Usually the victim would slump to his knees and point weakly to the far end of the queue so Grumpy would go off and investigate. This left the coast clear for a return snowball.

"Be quick!" I said anxiously. "There's people getting in line all the time."

"Shut up," said Pete. "He'll lose count." At last David Clifford had finished and we were in the queue.

"How many?" I demanded.

"We're in the hundred-and-sixties. That's the closest I can get."

"That's good enough," said Pete. "We're well inside."

We relaxed and nudged each other. In another two or three minutes the remaining places were taken. At the end of the queue a dozen-or-so latecomers stayed on, hoping they'd miscounted—or that Grumpy would when he started letting us in. He never did but there might be a first time.

"Think it'll be good?" I asked the kid behind me.

"Should be," he said. "See the trailer last week?"

"You bet!"

"The way he swung out of the rigging like that and landed on that bloke!"

"The way he beat those three men in the sword fight!"

"Cutlass fight," the kid corrected.

"Cutlass fight, then."

"That bit where he's clapped in irons by the other pirate!" added Pete.

"What about when he threw rum in his face!" said the kid.

"What did he do that for?" David Clifford asked.

"Do what for?"

"Why would he throw rum in his face?"

There was a moment's silence. Behind his glasses David Clifford was blinking in puzzlement. Slowly it dawned on us what he meant.

"He didn't throw rum in his *own* face, you goon," said the kid. "He threw it in the *other* pirate's face."

"Oh, I see." We howled with laughter and made when-do-they-take-him-away-faces at each other. We all felt good. Except David Clifford, maybe.

"Someone ought to do that to Fatty Rosewell," laughed the kid.

"What—throw rum in his face?" Pete said.

"And beat him in a cutlass fight," I added.

"Or jump out of the rigging on top of him," Pete went on.

"You'd bounce back," said the kid. "Better to clap him in irons. That's the best thing for Fatty Rosewell!"

"You talking about me?" asked Fatty Rosewell. We all spun round and froze.

Fatty had his hands in the pockets of his khaki windcheater. His legs, in his khaki trousers, were a little apart. He looked like a gorilla in a boy-scout uniform.

"Mush," he said. "I asked if you were talking about me."

The kid was too terrified to reply. He edged back against the wall. Fatty took a step forward.

"I asked you a question, Mush."

The kid shook his head but still said nothing. Fatty's hand shot out. He had the kid by the throat.

"What did you call me?" he hissed.

So tight was Fatty's grip the kid's voice could hardly get out.

"What did you say?"

"Nothing!"

"Don't lie to me, Mush. You called me Fatty, didn't you? Didn't you?"

13

By now the kid's face seemed to be turning blue. He was making coughing noises.

"You're strangling him!" Pete burst out. Fatty turned on him in a flash, releasing the kid.

"Do you want some?" he snarled.

"No."

"Then I suggest you mind yours, Mush."

He turned back to the kid, who was doubled up, trying not to be seen crying.

"You know it's all muscle now, Mush, don't you? Don't you!"

"Yes!" the kid half-gasped, half-sobbed.

"It's all muscle, Mush. Not fat. Muscle. So watch your lip in future."

Fatty swaggered back. He looked the group of us over. All of a sudden we had plenty of space.

"There's something wrong here ..." said Fatty, slowly. "One of you Mushes has got my place in the queue. Now who is it, I wonder ..."

The kid, who was now shivering, made a move to go.

"Not you, Mush," Fatty said. "Not you. You haven't got my place. You and me are going to have a little talk later on. No, it's one of these Mushes here ..." His eyes drifted over Pete and me. I felt my insides turn a slow somersault. More and more heads turned our way. Everyone was on our side, of course, but we knew no one would help us. And Grumpy was miles away. Fatty would have made sure of that. Pete licked his lips. I knew my brother was quite stubborn enough to get himself bashed up. I wasn't, though. I shrugged and began to work a half-smile onto my face to suggest I'd had my doubts about *The Crimson Pirate* as a film all along. We braced ourselves as Fatty sauntered forward.

Then David Clifford coughed.

Fatty's eyes flicked his way. A smirk spread over his face. You could see why when you looked at David Clifford. He was at his most weed-like. He looked all glasses and hair. He was shifting from one spindly leg to the other as if he was about to wet himself. On his head his school cap was much too small for him. Like a pea on a drum, Mum would have said.

"You, Mush," Fatty declared. "You got my place."

David Clifford blinked.

"Me?"

"Yes, you. Thanks for saving my place, Mush. I'll have it now."

"Not me. I haven't got your place."

"What?"

"This is my place. I got here first. I've been queuing."

"Look, Mush. If I say you've got my place, you've got my place. Now get out of my place, Mush."

"No," said David Clifford.

"No?" echoed Fatty.

He couldn't believe his ears. Neither could we. We all gaped at the pair of them but mostly at David Clifford. He'd blushed to the roots of his pimples and was blinking furiously. Otherwise he looked quite sane. When Fatty spoke

15

again it was with spine-chilling calm.

"Mush," he said. "I can have anything I want. Anything at all."

"Not my place."

"Anything," repeated Fatty.

He reached forward and took David Clifford's cap.

"Give that back!"

Fatty tossed the cap away from the queue.

"If you want it," he said, "go and get it."

"Then you'll pinch my place."

"That's right."

David Clifford was almost in tears with anger.

"You're just a great fat bully!" he exclaimed.

"A what!" Fatty roared.

"A great fat pig of a bully!"

Several kids gasped, including me. Slowly Fatty bunched his fists, curled his lip and thrust his chin forward.

"That does it, Mush," he said heavily. "I never start a fight. I finish 'em. Now hit me."

He tapped his chin with the knuckles of his clenched right hand.

"Hit me," he invited.

"What for?"

"You'll soon find out," Fatty grated. "Now hit me."

David Clifford blinked at the jutting chin. He was almost as tall as Fatty though he was two years younger. But he was a fraction as wide.

"Come on," snarled Fatty. "Hit me."

David Clifford actually seemed to be thinking about it. As a friend, I felt I had to give him some advice. I spoke out of the corner of my mouth and tried to keep my voice as cheerful as possible.

"He'll kill you," I said.

He didn't seem to hear.

"He'll kill him," I said to Pete.

"Hit me!" Fatty demanded.

Still David Clifford didn't make a move. Fatty's face twisted in a sneer. His mouth rounded, he fluted his tongue and spat. It hit David Clifford across the nose and mouth and clung like frogspawn. For a moment he stood rigid with disgust. Then he reacted.

"You fat Filth!" he screamed.

He bounded forward in a great kangaroo hop. His fist moved so fast we none of us saw the punch clearly. We saw Fatty's head snap backwards as it smashed into his face, though, and we saw Fatty fall flat on his back as if in slow-motion. He lay in the snow making weird snuffling moans. Blood covered his face. After a while he propped himself on his elbows but still didn't try to get up. He looked as if he was wearing a red gangster's mask. David Clifford was shaking as he rubbed at his mouth with his sleeve.

"Get off my cap," he whimpered.

Fatty took no notice.

"Get off my cap!" he repeated, his voice rising. "You're lying on it."

With a groan Fatty rolled aside. As David Clifford straightened up with the cap in his hand, Grumpy arrived.

He had been having a bad morning. Even his little white moustache was bristling.

"What's this?" he demanded. "Did you do this? Did you hit him?"

"Yes."

"Queue-jumping, I suppose."

"Yes."

"What!" exploded Grumpy. "You admit it, do you? You kids get worse and worse for brass. All right, son, all right. Have you got a handkerchief?"

He bent to help Fatty up. Even on his feet Fatty still looked dazed. He saw David Clifford lift his arm, though, and reeled backwards—cannoning into Grumpy.

"I saw that! I saw that!" Grumpy roared. "Just leave him alone, will you. You've done enough damage already. Broken his nose more than likely."

"I was only putting my cap on."

"Ho yes, 'course you were. 'E got that nose when you pulled your socks up, too, I suppose. Don't give me that! You keep those mitts of yours to yourself. It's okay, son, it's okay. I'll keep him off you. Your place is safe. I'll see you get inside for the film." David Clifford gasped.

"But it was him trying to grab my place!"

"Very likely," Grumpy scoffed. "Very likely, I'm sure. Look at that nose. You must think I'm dim. A moment ago you admitted yourself you were pushing in."

"I didn't."

"You lying little—I heard it with my own ears! Now you get off home."

"But I wasn't—"

"Off!"

"Listen—"

"No arguin'. It'll get you nowhere. Off home!" As David Clifford turned away, Pete found his voice.

"That's not fair. You've got it all wrong. Fatty was doing the pushing in and he hit him to save his place."

"Ho!" said Grumpy. "So he did hit him then."

"Yes, but—"

"Now we're getting the truth at last. Just now he was telling me he was only putting his cap on. He must think I'm dim."

"No, no!" Pete exclaimed. "He hit him before that."

"Before that? You mean he hit him twice? The little swine!"

"No!" howled Pete.

"Listen," I broke in, "you've got it all the wrong way round—"

"Another one!" spluttered Grumpy.

"Listen—" I began again.

"You listen to me instead, son," Grumpy snapped. "You must think I'm dim. Since you two are such good friends of his you can keep him company. Go on—off! All three of you. I've had enough of this. Off!"

"But—"

"Off! You say another word and so help me I'll call the manager and have you banned from the Cinema *permanent*."

The threat was enough. We turned away. We were stunned by the injustice of it. The shout of protest from the kids who'd seen the whole thing seemed far away. So did Grumpy's reply that they must think he was dim. Mechanically, we walked down the queue. Near the front, a kid stopped us.

"Going home?" he said. "What's up?"

"Chucked out," I said. "He bashed up Fatty Rosewell."

"Who him?" said the kid. He leaned out of his place and looked back. Fatty was still concussed. Grumpy was holding him up.

"Hey!" said the kid, "he bashed up Fatty Rosewell."

"What him?" said someone else. "Fatty Rosewell?"

"He's got blood all over him. Look up there if you don't believe me."

Others heard it and turned round. By the time we were over the road from the Odeon lots of kids were talking about it and pointing our way. Some of them had got it wrong, though. They thought it was Pete or me who'd done the bashing.

On the corner of College Slip we stopped.

"So much for *The Crimson Pirate*," said Pete. "What shall we do now?"

"The park?" I suggested. "Coming to the park, David?"

He shook his head.

"I'm going home. See you at school on Monday."

"Sure?" I asked.

He nodded.

"See you then," we said.

"See you."

We watched him go. By the time he got to College Road we could hardly make out his skimpy figure against the snow.

"Well that's your lot next week," sighed Pete.

"Huh?"

"You know what he'll do when he gets home?"

"No?"

"Practise his arithmetic."

I sprang at once but Pete was a much faster mover than Fatty Rosewell. We were at Martin's Hill, near the toboggans, before I caught up with him.

• Pokerface •

On a day like that, Jim's first problem was to keep his comics dry. The trees outside the school hissed with rain. Every inch of the playground threw up a blade of water. He tucked the comics inside his jacket, turned up his collar and darted for home. His second problem, he knew, would be his mum.

She was ironing when he got in.

"You'd better get that shirt off, Jimmy," she said at once. "Come here and let me dry your hair."

"I'll do it, Mum," Jim insisted.

"What have you got there?" she asked, suddenly.

Jim hesitated. "Comics," he said.

"What comics?"

"Swops with Kit and Pete Rowley."

"American comics? Like the ones last week? You know I don't like you reading that sort, Jimmy. All horror and fighting. Don't we buy you enough comics of your own?"

"I've read mine. Anyway I swopped them for these."

"Haven't you got a book you could read?"

"No," said Jim. "Everybody reads these. Go on, Mum. They're all right."

His mother thought of the rain outside and of the dark later and frowned as she picked up her ironing. "Just this once, then. But don't get any more like that from those Rowley twins. They're not good for you, Jimmy."

"Okay," said Jim, with relief.

As soon as he was dry, he slumped in the chair by the grate, perched his feet on the fender and opened the first of them.

"Reach up and put the wireless on," his mum said. "It's time for the fifteen-minute play."

Jim settled back, contentedly. For a few moments, he knew, the radio would overlap his reading. Then the sound would fade as *The Heap* and *Plasticman* and *Flash Gordon* took over.

This play was a bit longer going. When the theme music dissolved and the title had been announced, Jim heard footsteps on gravel—two people. The footsteps halted.

"What's that over there, darling?" said a smooth, actor's voice.

"Where?" asked a girl.

"Over there, by the hedge. It looks like a dog. An Alsatian."

"I see it," said the girl. "Is it asleep?"

"I don't know. There's something odd about the way it's lying ... I think it's ... dead. Look, I'd better go and see. Don't come with me. If it's been caught in a trap it'll be messy. You'll only get upset, darling."

"Michael—be careful!" the girl exclaimed.

"Of course I will. But we can't just leave it. If it is dead we ought to let the owners know. Might be an address or something on its collar. Don't look so worried, love! I'm quite sure it's dead, poor thing."

Then came one set of footsteps, through grass this time. Jim rustled his comic irritably. It annoyed him that he couldn't shut the radio out straight away. He wanted to concentrate on Flash Gordon who had a space monster to contend with—not a dead dog. He heard the actor playing Michael catch his breath.

"Good God!"

"What is it?" came the girl's voice, further off.

"Don't come over here! Stay there!"

"Michael, what is it?"

"It's horrible. The dog looks as if it's been—strangled! Its head's been twisted right back on its neck ..."

"Michael!" the girl screamed. "Behind you!"

Michael's exclamation of alarm was pitched just above the low, deep-throated laugh from the other side of the hedge. The footsteps over the grass were running this time—then both sets, on gravel, fading fast.

Jim shivered and tried to give Flash Gordon all his attention. Certainly he needed it. The monster was half the size of the solar-system with tentacles as long as the Milky Way. Enough to keep both Flash and Jim occupied. But Jim still heard the report at the police-station about the choked Alsatian and the huge, bald man behind the hedge who thought it was funny. He felt his mother's eyes on him.

"Is that radio too loud for you, Jimmy?"

"Huh?"

"The radio. Is it too loud?"

"No, Mum. Can't hear it."

"Are you sure?"

Jim held up his comic enthusiastically.

"There's this monster, Mum, who's swallowed Venus and it's devouring space and Flash Gordon's got to stop it. Great!" He turned over and fixed his eyes on the next page. His mother watched him a moment. He was glad when she started ironing again.

They took the dog away. The vet confirmed that it had been strangled. But who, or what, could strangle a fully-grown Alsatian? No one knew. Of the bald laugher there was no trace. The old lady in the cottage nearby didn't know who he could be. Hers was the only house in the lane, she said. No one came here. Except courting couples, sometimes.

Jim knew the old lady was lying. You didn't have to be Flash Gordon to see that. It was in her voice, and the way she slipped the catch on the door after the sergeant had gone. She was muttering as she shuffled into her parlour. A chair scraped and there was the scratch of a nib on paper. The old lady read aloud as she wrote.

"He got out today. I must be more careful. His restless spells come more and more often.

It's difficult to control him, even with the poker. He'll only do what I say because of the poker. He's terrified of that, still. But when will he talk to me again? It's so long since he talked to me."

The old lady on the radio sighed.

Jim shifted his feet and strained to read the comic. If the monster ate any more planets, the balance of the solar system would be upset, scientists declared. It all depended on Flash, who made his preparations carefully. A new rocket-ship, heavily-armed, had to be designed and built, to Flash's specifications. Every second counted, but things couldn't be rushed. By the time all was ready ... he heard the old lady again, chuckling over her diary.

"The funny thing is," she read out, "the poker isn't hot at all. It's just red paint at the end of it. I stopped lighting the fire two months ago at the beginning of the summer. He can't tell the difference. To him it's as frightening as the one I burnt him with. That was a piece of luck! He was getting too much for me. He obeys me now, like he used to."

Her voice changed. She added a sentence, pronouncing each word as she finished it. "If-only-he-still-talked-to-me ..."

A drink of water—that's what I need, Jim thought. He stood up, laying the comic face downwards on the chair, as if not wanting to lose his place.

"Mind the flex on the iron," his mother said sharply.

Jim stepped over it and crossed the kitchen.

The spatter of water in the sink cut him off from the old lady and the big, bald man she sheltered. He didn't want to turn off the tap. He heard his mother say something. Reluctantly, he reached for the tap.

"What did you say?' he asked.

"I said are you going to have a bath there, or what?"

"Oh," said Jim sheepishly. "I was thinking." By the time he was sitting down again holding the comic three inches from his face, the dryness was back in his throat.

Over the air came the creak of floor-boards. The bald man was pacing his bedroom, backwards and forwards. Then he began to throw himself against the locked door. Several sound-effects followed—the old lady's footsteps on the stairs, the poker catching the banister, the splintering wood of the door on the landing. Then a key in a lock.

"Stand back!" said the old lady, sharply. "I've got the poker here. See it? Do you want it to burn you again? They've just come here about you, they have. What did you do to that dog? Eh? Answer me! Haven't you got a tongue in your head? No, you'd rather use those hands of yours wouldn't you—on dogs, or people, or even me. I know your moods. One more trick like today's and you'll feel this poker again. Like last time!"

Jim's stomach suddenly went cold. He was good at guessing how stories would turn out. Miss Hart, his teacher, had said so. Often he knew what was going to happen ahead of Flash

Gordon, himself. He saw now how this story was going to turn out. He saw the old lady jab the poker just a little too far. He saw its tip brush against the skin without burning it and the frozen moment when they both realized what had happened. Then he saw the bald laugher's hands beginning to twitch, beginning to reach. Jim was way ahead of the radio-play. It still had several scenes to go. But for Jim it was all over.

"Jimmy, dear," his mother broke in, "would you run upstairs for me?"

"What?"

"Would you run upstairs and get your father's trousers for me? They need pressing. They're on the chair by the dressing table."

"What?"

"Your father's trousers. Upstairs on the chair by the dressing table."

"Oh yes. Okay, Mum."

In a rush, he was out of the kitchen, through the living room and had closed its door behind him. He stood in the hall and shut his eyes, waiting for the sledgehammer in his chest to stop pounding. What was it Mum had wanted? If he went back and asked, she'd only tease him about being an absent-minded professor. And he might hear more of the play. He shuddered. Something about the dressing table, was it? Trying to remember, he started up the stairs.

The frosted Victorian glass at the end of the passage kept the hall dark, but Jim didn't bother to switch on the light. He knew every stair from its creak. He nipped up them like a cat.

Halfway, he stopped—Dad's trousers from the chair by the dressing table, that was it. Pleased with himself he looked up. The bedroom door where the stairs turned was wide open. Within was the bright shape of the window beaded with rain. And outlined clearly against it was the curve of a bald-head, the slope of a shoulder: Poker-face.

Jimmy went rigid. Any second, he expected the laugh. Or would that only come ... afterwards? He suddenly found he could scream. He screamed.

Below him the door jerked open. "Jimmy, whatever's the matter?" exclaimed his Mum. He wouldn't say. For ten minutes, sitting next to him on the stairs, she cuddled him until he stopped shivering. There was nothing in the hall to frighten him. All you could see from that position was the open door of the bedroom and the window beyond it where the light-fitting hung and a flared curtain was half-drawn. She gave up questioning him after a while.

"I think it's stopped raining, Jimmy," she said, when they were in the kitchen again. "Go to the back door and look."

"It has, Mum," he said.

"Why don't you put your mac and boots on and play in the garden for a bit? Till your father gets home. It's not really dark yet."

"I don't want to."

"Please yourself."

She shook her head in puzzlement. Sometimes it seemed to her she understood her eight-year-old less and less.

"You're not going to read those comics, Jimmy," she added, firmly.

"Oh, Mum!"

"No. That's definite. Not after just now. Would you like the radio back on?"

"No!"

"It's no use sulking, Jimmy. You're not having those comics. So make your mind up what you're going to do."

Miserably, Jimmy looked out at the wet, darkening garden. Next door's fence was easily big enough to have a bald laugher behind it. And round the corner by the coalshed, the grass could be cluttered with dead Alsatians. Now he couldn't even read about Flash Gordon. He could always write to him, though. Jimmy perked up. They'd done letter-writing at school last week. He'd write to Flash Gordon and find out if he had a place in his crew for someone who could see as far ahead as Jimmy could. Not straight away, of course. In about five years time, say. Space monsters were different. Miss Hart would know the address.

"Mum," he asked, "have we got any letter-writing paper? Can I have some?"

"Yes dear. It's in the sideboard."

Trying not to look at next door's fence, Jimmy shut the back door.

· An Oscar for Godfrey ·

He was a born actor. Everybody told him that.

"Godfrey Fanshaw, you're a born actor," his last teacher had said.

Godfrey had sniffed as if he couldn't care less. But this wasn't true—he wanted to be an actor more than anything else in the world. He practised all the time.

Even Godfrey's Mum recognized his acting talent though she wasn't always enthusiastic about it. "Run round the shops for me, Godfrey—and spare us the agony," she'd add, before he could work a pained expression onto his face. Still, one day she'd be his most loyal fan. He was sure of that. She'd regret nasty little misunderstandings like the one that had happened this morning.

Jimmy, from up the street, had called for him early to swop comics. They'd got into an argument when Jimmy insisted that two copies of *Beano* equalled one *Plasticman*. In the end Godfrey was forced to hit him. As Jimmy lay blubbering at his feet, Godfrey played it exactly the way Marlon Brando had, on television, the night before.

"Get up you scum-sucking pig," he snarled. "Get up!"

The next thing he knew he'd been knocked sideways. A storm of cuffs and punches and slaps broke over his head and shoulders. It was his mum.

"How-many-times-have-I-told-you-there'll-be -no-swearing-in-this-house!" she screamed between blows.

"Is your mum always like that about swearing?" Jimmy asked on the way to school.

"Always," said Godfrey bitterly.

"What—every kind of swearing?"

"Every kind."

Jimmy giggled.

"She wouldn't much like my dad, then!"

"Why? What does he say?"

"Well, it's not really swearing," said Jimmy cagily. "He says it's more a turn of phrase."

"What is?"

"I'd better not tell you. I don't want to get you into trouble with your mum."

"She won't know, will she. Come on, tell us."

"Better not."

Godfrey gritted his teeth like Humphrey Bogart.

"All right, all right," Jimmy said hastily. "He says it when I'm looking fed up. You know—got a downcast look on my face."

"Says *what*?"

"I'm telling you. He says 'Cor Jim, you've

got a face like a smacked arse'!"

"What!"

"That's what he says—'a face like a smacked arse'. It's not really swearing. It's a turn-of-phrase."

"Sounds like it!" Godfrey exclaimed.

"My Dad would probably say it right now about your face," Jimmy said.

Godfrey altered his expression quickly.

His sour look came back fast though once he was in the classroom. It was her—Miss Dixon. Godfrey didn't like her one bit. When Miss Manly had told the kids she was handing over to a student this term they'd heaved a sigh of relief. No one could be stricter than Old Mother Manly, they thought. Especially a student. Then Miss Dixon arrived. She was as pretty as a film-star and as tough as a stunt-man. And she wanted a distinction for her teaching-practice, it was said. For six weeks she'd worked them harder than they'd ever worked before. Worse than that she even made them *enjoy* work. Godfrey resented it deeply. After all, reading and writing were okay for script-writers but he was going to be an actor. Thank goodness today was her last day.

"Good—everyone here," said Miss Dixon, closing the register. "Now line up in twos outside, please."

"Line up?" Godfrey asked Kate, who sat next to him. "What for?"

"Swimming. It's Friday. Don't you know what day it is?"

"I forgot."

"Haven't you got your swimming things?"

"How could I if I forgot?"

Kate rolled her eyes.

"You've had it! Remember what she said to you last time. She said you'd go to Miss Gregg if it happened again."

"She wouldn't. It's her last day. She's all talk."

"Glad you think so. Glad it's not me who's forgotten my swimming things three weeks in a row, that's all I can say."

"She's all talk," Godfrey insisted.

"You won't mind me telling her then, will you? Miss!"

"Shut up!" Godfrey hissed.

"Miss!"

"Yes, Kate?"

"I thought I'd remind you, Miss. You said ... you said we'd do some handwriting for Monday's Parents' Evening."

"That's right. I've planned it for this afternoon. Hurry up, now. Miss Manly will be waiting in the lobby."

"See you on the coach, Godfrey!" said Kate sweetly.

Godfrey stood up.

"Where are your swimming things?" Miss Dixon asked at once.

Godfrey shrugged just the way Charles Bronson did.

"Godfrey Fanshaw—you *haven't*. Not three weeks in a row! What did I tell you last time?"

"Don't remember."

"I said you'd go straight to Miss Gregg. You

mustn't write swimming off just because you don't like the instructor. I know you got into trouble the first week. You were fooling about— pretending you were Tarzan or something. That's dangerous in a swimming-bath. He has to be strict. You behave yourself and you'll get on with him all right. And you'll learn to swim. Don't you want to swim?"

"Don't need to," said Godfrey. "They have extras for that. Stand-ins."

"Sorry? What did you say, Godfrey?"

"Doesn't matter," said Godfrey wearily. "I just forgot, okay?"

"No, it is *not* okay. And I haven't forgotten what I said I'd do about it, either. It's the headmistress for you, my lad. Everyone else lead on down to Miss Manly. No messing about, please. Come on, Godfrey."

"Goodbye, Godfrey,' called Kate.

Godfrey's walk along the corridor was an exact copy of James Cagney's down Death Row. Miss Dixon, beside him, didn't even notice. Probably she went to bed too early for the Midnight Movie.

"... I see," said Miss Gregg. She had been looking at Godfrey sorrowfully while Miss Dixon explained. Godfrey shifted his feet. He was never quite sure of Miss Gregg. Once she'd told a story in assembly about a play she'd acted in. Perhaps she'd been in films, too. You could never tell with Miss Gregg.

"What's your explanation, Godfrey?" she asked.

"Don't know."

35

"It's a school rule about swimming. We can't afford to give you a choice about that. Too many people are drowned every year. What would you do if you were drowning?"

"Shout for help."

"Suppose the person you were shouting to had never learned to swim?"

"I'd drown."

"I see. And what if someone else drowned trying to save you? How would you feel about that?" This was an awkward question to answer like many of Miss Gregg's questions. Godfrey felt uneasy—sick almost. Serve her right if he fainted. Then she'd be sorry. Miss Dixon, too. They'd both be sorry if he fainted. He began to sway gently to get them started. He screwed up his eyes and gave his head a shake as if trying to clear it. Any second now one of them would ask him if he was all right.

"I know," said Miss Gregg brightly. "We could arrange a transfer. To a school nowhere near any water—right away from the sea, rivers, canals, ponds and so on. There must be one somewhere in England. The Divisional Officer will know. You'll be quite safe there. So will anyone else who might otherwise have to rescue you. What a good idea!"

She must be blind as a bat, Godfrey thought. He gave a low, hollow groan. She couldn't be deaf, too.

"Manners, Godfrey," she said disapprovingly. "Did you have baked beans for breakfast, dear? Let me just dial the Divisional Office number and see ... ah, hello Divisional Officer? Miss

Gregg here. I've a lad with me—Godfrey Fanshaw—who'd like a transfer. He disagrees with
the school rule about swimming. Do you know
of any schools in England right away from all
water? You do? Splendid! Can you give me the
details?"

Godfrey could hardly believe it. Here he was
dying on his feet and she hadn't even noticed!
Nor had Miss Dixon. She seemed to be staring
out of the window. They were just as bad as
his mum, the pair of them. Something spectacular was called for, he could see that. He
slumped at the knees and flung himself on the
floor, arms outspread. His head was on one
side, his eyes were shut fast and one of his legs
was bent. D'Artagnan had fallen like that in *The
Three Musketeers*. He lay still, expecting Miss
Gregg to rush off at once for the first-aid box.
Instead, she went on talking.

"I'm not sure if he can speak to you now,
Divisional Officer, he seems to be resting. Shall
I get him to phone you back a little later? And
you'll begin making the arrangements? Excellent.
Goodbye for now. It's all right, Godfrey, don't
get up if you're feeling tired. The Divisional
Officer will fix everything. Why are you lying
in that peculiar position, dear? There's no need
for you to practise your swimming-strokes now."

Get up? Godfrey had no intention of getting
up. Without help, anyway. He couldn't understand what had gone wrong. His groan this
time was almost genuine. Perhaps he should
try a death-rattle ...

"I believe he's snoring," Miss Gregg said.

"Don't wake him, Miss Dixon. He'll need all his strength for the journey. It's a long way to his new school. Let him sleep. Come next door into the office. We'll have a chat. Today's your last day, I believe. You're hoping for a Distinction, aren't you?"

Miss Dixon didn't answer. In fact she hadn't said a word for some time now. She'd been making an odd, spluttering noise. She was making it now as she left the room behind Miss Gregg. It couldn't be ... could it? Slowly Godfrey sat up. His cheeks were scarlet. Miss Dixon had actually been *laughing*. At him.

For the rest of the morning, at lunchtime and all afternoon he plotted vengeance. She was to blame—Miss Dixon. He wouldn't have gone to Miss Gregg in the first place if it hadn't been for her. He wouldn't have been out-acted. For the more he thought about it, the more he knew he'd been conned. Transfer to a school nowhere near any water! There wasn't any such place. Anyway, he'd bring his swimming things next week. Every time he thought of his collapse in Miss Gregg's room he wanted to crawl into the inkwell on his desk and slide the lid shut after him. There must be some way he could get his own back—but how?

By the last lesson of the day—the last lesson Miss Dixon would ever teach them—he still hadn't come up with anything. On the blackboard she'd pinned a picture of a fishing-boat in difficulties.

"Now look at the picture carefully," she was saying. "I want us all to write a paragraph together that's really extra-special. We'll copy it

38

out in our best handwriting as we go along. Remember it's for the Parents' Evening on Monday. It'll be on display with your maths work and your paintings and your project-folders. I only wish I could be there myself. Who's going to start us off with a really exciting sentence? Teddy?"

"The sea is very rough," Teddy suggested.

"It is, too," Miss Dixon agreed. "Look at those waves! And the angle of the ship! Can anyone improve on Teddy's sentence? I want something dynamic and thrilling—something that will really make the reader sit up. Now rack your brains everyone. Kate?"

"The sea seems to have gone mad."

"That's much more dramatic! Shall we start with that? Kit?"

"This is the Devil's Sea!"

"Marvellous, Kit!" Miss Dixon exclaimed. "What a marvellous sentence. My goodness we'll have our work cut out to follow that! Let's write it up. Careful, beautiful copying please ... don't rush ... it's so easy to make a mistake when you're thinking about your handwriting. Good! 'This is the Devil's Sea.' Who's got an idea for the next sentence?"

Godfrey yawned elaborately. He glanced at the clock. For once its hands seemed to be galloping towards home-time. Was it already too late? He couldn't even muck up the handwriting since his own mum would be coming to Parents' Evening and would practically look through a magnifying-glass at every piece of work he'd done. As the seconds ticked away and sentence followed sentence on the black-board he began to despair.

Soon Miss Dixon was reading through the passage. And rather over-acting it seemed to Godfrey.

"This is the Devil's Sea. The waves roar, the gulls screech. Cr-a-a-ack! Lightning zig-zags across the dark, misty water. In the ship's hold fish wriggle and thresh and squirm and slowly die. The ocean is giant troughs. Fishermen have an exciting and terrifying life. Foam sprays across the salty deck. The Captain's face looks like ..."

Godfrey held his breath. In a flash he saw forty neat copies pinned to the display-board, along with their maths work and their paintings and their project-folders. He saw forty sets of mums and dads storming off to Miss Gregg's office to complain. He saw his own mum among them. She would be too furious to listen to any explanation. "Typical cover-up job," she'd say. Anyway, Miss Dixon wouldn't be there to explain. Today was her last day. And it would ruin her chance of a Distinction. His hand shot up.

"Godfrey? Fine!" said Miss Dixon. "You haven't given us any ideas so far. Now bring it to a stunning finish, Godfrey. The Captain's face looks like ..."

"... a smacked arse," Godfrey said.

Someone gasped. Miss Dixon turned slowly from the blackboard, the chalk poised in her hand.

" *What* did you say?"

"A smacked arse," Godfrey repeated. The whole class waited with pens hovering. The next bit would be the tricky bit, he knew. He'd have to get his voice just right.

"It's a turn-of-phrase," he explained. "My mum uses it. When I'm looking fed up she says, 'Cor, Godfrey, you've got a face like a smacked arse.' Like the Captain, Miss. I mean, I'd be fed up if it was my ship getting smashed to pieces."

"Of course," he added, shyly. "I shan't mind if you don't want to use it because it's sort of—well, sort of rude, Miss. I know it's for Parents' Evening and that. It's what my mum says ..." His voice trailed off. He bit his lip and lowered his eyes.

"Nonsense, Godfrey," said Miss Dixon briskly, pulling herself together. "What's good enough for your mum is good enough for me. I think it's a super phrase. Just right. Certainly we'll use it. A lot of people in this class come into school on a Monday morning with faces like ... like ... er ... smacked arses. Copy it please, children." Turning to the blackboard she finished off the sentence with a flourish. Forty hands followed hers, slavishly. Three words of handwriting, at least, would be perfect.

It was Godfrey's greatest performance. He was awestruck at his own brilliance. She'd fallen head-first into his trap. Gleefully he pictured his mum's expression when she saw it. Already he could hear her voice, shrill with outrage, telling their next-door neighbour. He looked up in time to catch Miss Dixon's smile as she went on talking and writing.

"We must give the credit to the person who invented the phrase, though. That's only fair. Put quotation-marks round the last three words, everyone, like this. And add the author's name in brackets: Godfrey Fanshaw's mum. I'll ask Miss Manly to thank Godfrey's mum on Monday for finishing off our paragraph for us so splendidly." Thirty-nine hands added quotation-marks and the name and brackets. The fortieth was Godfrey's. He felt like Count Dracula in the horror film when the wooden stake has been hammered into his heart. He was in the same frozen position when school ended.

· Wednesday's Werewolf ·

It was a house that gave you the creeps. Somehow it didn't fit in with the rest of the street. It should have been a woodyard, or a laundry, or flats. But there it was ... looking empty but for the smoke that curled thinly from a chimney-cowl. The trees in the front garden were all wrong, too. On one side their branches crowded the verandah, on the other they were clipped by the traffic. Beneath them, the dirt path that led to the front door was deep in shadow.

As soon as Teddy and Pete saw it they knew the usual knock-at-the-door-and-run-away wasn't good enough. This house called for something extra.

"Fancy letting it get in that state," said Teddy. "Bet the neighbours aren't too pleased."

He nodded at the broken slates on the grass. They were standing at a gap in the railings where the gate should have been.

"Hasn't really got any neighbours," Pete pointed out.

Uphill, beyond a corrugated iron fence, was a dump for scrap-metal. Downhill the row of shops continued.

"It's just right then," said Teddy thoughtfully.

"What?"

"For a special kind of knock-down-ginger. Listen, I've thought of a new twist." He pulled Pete to one side where the trees screened them. Then he began to whisper.

"You see?" he said finally. "It's easy. And this way we get to see who we're making a fool of!"

"We couldn't make it convincing," Pete protested.

"Course we could."

"Couldn't we just knock and run like always?"

"Don't be such a scaredycat."

"It's too risky."

"Okay then, scaredycat," Teddy sighed. "I'll do the knocking on my own this time, you join in with the other part. I'll even do the talking as we walk past. Okay? All you've got to do is put one foot in front of the other. Think you can manage that?"

"I suppose so," said Pete, reluctantly.

"Right. Stay here. I'll only be a second." Off he dashed. Pete bit his lip. If only Teddy wouldn't get these mad ideas. He always took things one step too far.

Teddy scampered back just as a lorry passed, setting the leaves and shadows in a flurry. Pete shivered.

"Come on," Teddy hissed. "I knocked really loud."

They started walking. Teddy kept the pace almost to a saunter. At the same time he talked, his voice rather high-pitched.

"Nice weather we're having," he said. "Have you been away yet? I haven't either. We can't afford it this year. Prices are terrible aren't they. Don't know what the government's up to. They're all the same, politicians. That's what my Dad always says ..."

Level with the gap in the railings, both boys glanced at the house. The front-door was wide open. Before they'd looked away it had shut again. The boys blinked and stared at each other. Then they started to run. They were past the shops before they slowed down.

"Stop!" Pete gasped. "I've got a stitch."

Teddy pressed his side and bent double to catch his breath.

"Stupid," he said at last.

"What?"

"Us—stupid. Why run like that? He'd already shut the front door. And anyway he couldn't exactly have chased us, could he?'

"Not wearing armour," Pete said.

Teddy smiled crookedly.

"It was armour, wasn't it? I thought for a minute I was seeing things. But it was armour?"

"It was armour," Pete insisted. "He was wearing armour." For half a minute they were silent, wide-eyed. If they quit now they could never call themselves daredevils again. They'd be scaredycats forever. There was only one thing they could do. Even Pete saw that.

"We've ... we've got to go back," he admitted.

"This time we'll both knock," Teddy said. "And we'll walk uphill so it looks like our return journey."

"Suppose he guesses it's us?"

"We'll challenge him to a joust!"

"We haven't got a horse."

"I'll borrow my dad's motorbike," Teddy suggested. "You can sit in the side-car with a clothes-prop for a lance."

"And a dustbin lid for a shield," giggled Pete. Feeling better, they started back. As they got closer the joke wore off, though. The sun on the opposite pavement was dazzling but the house's kerbstones were dark. Under the trees, they hesitated.

"After three then," said Teddy. "Okay?"

"Okay."

"You count."

"No, you."

Teddy licked his lips.

"All right, scaredycat, I'll count," he said. "But you've got to come with me."

"Course," said Pete, doubtfully.

"Ready? Here we go. One ... two ..."

On three both boys darted forward. Four paces brought them to the gap in the railings, six more took them onto the verandah. Together they lifted the knocker and banged it down. It sounded like the last nail hammered into a coffin-lid. They scuttled for safety, nearly colliding with each other at the railings.

Hidden by trees again, they smoothed themselves for their stroll. Teddy began talking.

"See what I mean?" he said. "The prices in those shop windows. Pretty soon it'll get so you can't afford to eat. Not that that will bother the rich people. They'll be all right as usual. My Dad says half the country is owned by ..."

Their heads turned at precisely the same moment.

There he was. In full armour. He leant against the woodwork with a gauntlet on his hip and one plated leg crossed over the other. The plume on his helmet was bent by the door-lintel. They heard him say something but the lowered visor muffled his voice. Then he beckoned them.

"Shall we go?" Teddy whispered.

Pete nodded vigorously. When Teddy turned up the dirt path Pete gaped with astonishment. He thought Teddy had meant go *home*. Swallowing hard, he forced himself to follow.

The man was fiddling with the visor. Eventually it scraped up. His eyes, suddenly revealed, were so watery they seemed to be afloat.

"Blasted thing," he remarked. "Gets stuck. Needs oiling. Must make a note of that." He peered down at Teddy and Pete.

"Just called you over, little gents, to tell you you didn't fool me for a minute. That whoever-knocked-on-your-door-it-wasn't-me-routine is as old as the hills. Spotted it at once. Used it myself as a kid."

"On ... on drawbridges?" Pete stammered.

"Eh? Drawbridges? Oh! You mean the King Arthur bit."

He threw back his head so far into the helmet his guffaw of laughter echoed slightly. Now they were close they could see the armour wasn't quite his size. It squeaked and rattled as he moved. The chain-mail beneath it sagged in places like an old sweater.

"Here," he said. "This'll put you in the picture." He took off a gauntlet and from somewhere amongst the metalwork produced a small white card. It read: "Magnus Period Pieces —Costumes and Properties for the Theatre".

"I'm Magnus," he announced.

"Sir Magnus," Teddy said.

"What? Oh—see what you mean, young gent. Quite correct. Of the Round Table, eh? Now then ... ah ..."

He seemed to be trying to make up his mind. His eyes, which were all they could see of him, flicked from one boy to the other, like fish in twin tanks.

"Er ... would you like, perhaps, to come inside and see the rest of my stock?" he said eventually. Even Teddy hesitated. They didn't like his eyes. They didn't like the sound of him either. His voice was hoarse with years of cigarette-smoke.

"Hmm ..." said Magnus. "Thinking of your mothers, I expect. Bit of a problem there. Probably warned you about accepting invitations from strange men. Quite right, too. Wouldn't they make an exception, though, for a knight in ... er ... shining armour? I can hardly move in this damn tackle, after all."

The boys exchanged a glance.

"Okay," said Teddy. "But we can't stay long."

"Thank you," he remembered to add.

Magnus was right about the armour. It made him lurch like a drunk robot. Helping him through the door, Pete asked, "Why do you put it on?"

"Best way to test it. Might be hired at any time. Got to make sure it's in working order, tip-top shape. Bad for business if it falls to bits at a rehearsal. I test all my stuff—do it on a rota: Monday is wigs and make-up; Tuesday is armour; Wednesday is special-effects; Thursday is ceremonial" But they weren't really listening. What they saw had all their attention.

The front door opened onto a staircase. This led down to a vast, dim room like a cave with floor-boards. It was filled with Magnus's stuff—on shelves, in boxes and cupboards or just piled up. It was like leftovers from history or Hollywood.

"Do you test those?" Pete asked.

He pointed. Against a wall was a rack of uniforms still glamorous beneath the dust.

"Formal dress," said Magnus. "For upper-crust officers, eighteenth century to the present day. "Can't say I do test them, no. There you have me. Perhaps—perhaps you two would care to test them for me? Slip them on over your clothes, of course. No need to catch cold, eh?"

"Could we?" Pete exclaimed.

"Certainly you can."

"Suppose we damaged them?" Teddy asked.

"Damage them? You wouldn't do that, would

you? Course not. Here—d'you like these?" He disappeared behind some shelving. When he came back he was buckling a gunbelt over his armour, complete with holsters, colts and cartridges.

"What do you think?"

"The fastest draw in Camelot," Pete giggled.

"Look out of place, of course," Magnus agreed. "Perfectly authentic in themselves, though."

"They're marvellous," said Teddy. "Can we go down and try on the uniforms now, please?"

"Certainly," Magnus said. "Go ahead."

His appearance as two-gun Galahad set the pattern for the rest of the afternoon. He kept interrupting them. Once he stepped from behind a screen with a gorilla-mask in place of his helmet. They nearly jumped out of their skins. Later he clanked down some steps with a clown's face. Then he made himself up like a Chinaman, with slant-eyes, pigtail and a coolie's hat. He became Black-beard the Pirate and Dracula and an Apache Indian and a Thing from Outer Space. But only as far as the neck. Always below was the armour.

"I wish he'd leave us alone," whispered Teddy fiercely. "We're not going to get through half these uniforms."

"If you ask me he's a bit dippy," Pete hissed. "Did you see the way he bent down on one knee when I saluted him? As if he was a *real* knight!"

Worst of all was when Magnus just sat and watched them from behind his visor. They marched and presented arms as best they could but it put them right off. At five o'clock they decided they'd better be going.

"Could we come back tomorrow," Teddy asked, "and test the rest of them for you?"

"Tomorrow?" said Magnus.

His filmy eyes shifted.

"Er ... no, not tomorrow, gents," he said with an effort. "Got a rota to keep to, you know, things to do, things to set up. Tell you what though—how about the same time next week? Next Tuesday. That any good?"

"That's nearly the end of the holidays," Teddy pointed out. "Couldn't we make it a bit sooner?" Magnus coughed and seemed to be deciding.

"Ah ... no," he said eventually. "Not on. Can't be done. Sorry and all that."

Teddy and Pete hid their disappointment.

"Fine," they said politely. "Next Tuesday, then. Goodbye."

"Soppy twit," said Teddy as soon as they couldn't be heard. "What's wrong with tomorrow? He's not going to be doing anything, is he—except testing his stupid costumes. Doesn't make any difference to him if we're there or not. We wouldn't be getting in his way. Next Tuesday we're back at school, practically."

"Those outfits ..." Pete sighed.

"We'll go back tomorrow," said Teddy firmly.

"What?"

"Tomorrow afternoon. He might have changed his mind."

"Isn't that a bit ... well, rude?"

"Rude? What about him, then—all that staring at us. That's rude isn't it? Staring?"

"Yes it is. But he did say Tuesday."

"He can say it again tomorrow then. Won't cost him anything, will it?"

"No," said Pete doubtfully.

"So see you tomorrow afternoon," Teddy insisted.

But by the next day Teddy himself had doubts. Partly it was the change in the weather. The sky was solid with cloud and there was a hint of rain in the wind. They stared at the house uneasily. It seemed to crouch behind the trees. One of its shutters creaked and banged.

"Come on, then," Teddy said.

"You first. It was your idea not to wait."

"Scaredycat," scoffed Teddy.

On the verandah they paused.

"Let's leave it," Pete begged.

Teddy shook his head and reached for the knocker. Before he could lift it they heard a noise from inside.

It started as a snuffle but changed to a low sucking snarl. Afterwards came a gnawing of bone and the rasp of haunches against woodwork. They felt the hair on their necks bristle.

"Teddy!" Pete gasped. "It's coming up the stairs!"

"Look at the window," said Teddy.

At the window they saw a face. It had fur and whiskers and teeth, with eyes that slanted wetly beneath pointed ears. Inch by inch, holding their breath, Pete and Teddy backed down the verandah steps. Once they were on the dirt path they turned and ran.

On the way home it started to rain. It rained all week and at the weekend. The following Tuesday it was still raining.

"Throw another stone," Teddy said.

"That's six," said Pete, "counting the two that didn't hit the door. He must have heard them. The last one was enough to wake the dead."

"He'll have his armour on, remember. It's Tuesday."

"Not sure I want him to hear," Pete admitted.

"There's nothing to worry about," Teddy insisted. "I keep telling you. It was a special-effect. Like for horror films and so on. He told us that was on Wednesday."

"Why are we staying out on the pavement then?" Pete asked.

They huddled under Teddy's duffle coat. The verandah roof had so many leaks the house looked as if it were melting. It had a dank smell. Even the trees seemed to be rotting away.

"Who's that?" Teddy exclaimed.

On the corner where the shops began a man was waving to them. Perhaps it was Magnus without his armour. He had to go out *sometime* after all. They ducked under the branches and went to see.

It wasn't Magnus. It was the newsagent from the first shop.

"What are you lads doing there?" he demanded. "That house is empty. The owner's gone."

"Gone?" asked Teddy. "Gone where?"

"Are you relatives or something?"

"No. We only met him once."

"Well you won't meet him again. He's been put away. In a home. And about time too if you ask me. Doodle-alley, he was. Him and his fancy-dress. Didn't know whether he was Bonny Prince Charlie or Scott of the Frozen North. And not just clothes either—a one-man bloody menagerie. Had the women round here scared stiff. Wouldn't let their kids go near his place. The trouble he's caused! Police came for him in the end. Here ... how come you two met him? Where are you going? Hey! I'm talking to you"

Teddy and Pete walked briskly, dodging the puddles. They didn't want details of the trouble Magnus had caused. It was bad enough that he'd been put away, even if they hadn't liked him very much.

"What'll happen to his costumes and things?" asked Pete. "Will they be kept for him till he's let out?"

Teddy shrugged.

"And we never saw his real face," Pete went on. "He never showed it once."

"Maybe he's showing it now," Teddy said.

• Ice •

In some places the snow was no thicker than a finger but in others it came higher than a wellington boot. Whichever it was Jimmy hated it.

It wasn't even white any more—not all over anyway. Some of it was just slush. This was caused by feet that crunched through it and hands that scooped it together for throwing. And toboggans.

Toboggans had worn it away most of all. Including Jimmy's toboggan. If you could call the thing *Jimmy's* toboggan. Teddy's toboggan more like. Or maybe Teddy-Pete-and-Kit's toboggan. Anybody would think *their* dad had made it. Anybody would think it belonged to *them* or to some kid who'd lent it out for the day. You wouldn't think it belonged to Jimmy. How could it belong to Jimmy when he was the only one who got scared? Jimmy was sick of the toboggan and sick of the snow and most of all he was sick of being Jimmy.

He looked around him miserably. Martin's Hill was different from the park where they usually went. Their normal park was vast and flat like a pitch for people with seven-league football boots. Also it was safe ... unlike Martin's Hill. Martin's Hill had a slope that took you to breakneck speed before you could even catch your breath. It had ledges and dips and gullies. It had stretches of ice like a skid-pan with trees and lamp-posts as obstacles. Martin's Hill was a somersaulting, head-on collision-course for mad kids on runaway sledges.

So why was he the *only* kid who got frightened?

He thought of Teddy. Teddy crouched on the toboggan jockey-style and treated each ride as if it were a frost-bitten Grand National which he just managed to win in the final furlong. Pete lay back like a racing-driver. Even Kit skimmed the ground, flat-out.

Still, at least for the moment Teddy and Pete and Kit were out of sight over the hill. They had stared after him when he stomped off.

"Hey, where are you going?" Pete called. "It's your turn, Jimmy."

"He's just going to the bog," suggested Teddy.

"The bog?" Kit exclaimed. "What—just before his turn?"

Jimmy hadn't heard Teddy's reply. If he made a reply. Probably already they were arguing over who took his place on the toboggan. On *his* toboggan. But if it was his toboggan why was he in such a funk about it?

They were older than him, of course. In two or three years' time maybe he would be just as reckless ... maybe. Anyway, in a day or two the snow would be gone and the problem would be over ... until the roller-skating season started or tree-climbing began or it came round to summer and jumping off the top board at the swimmingpool. Each of these left him dizzy with fear.

Perhaps you were just born brave. Or perhaps being brave was something you could get good at bit by bit. Like today ... was there some small risk he could take which he could build on gradually till by next winter it really would be his toboggan? There were no kids on this side of the slope. It was steep and long but too straightforward to be popular for tobogganing. Once you were at the bottom it took an age to get back to the top. Also the slope ended at the boating pool.

In summer the pool was overhung with leaves and full of coloured rowing-boats and pedal-boats and canoes like dodgem-cars in a floating fun-fair. These vanished in the autumn. Teddy said the park-keepers buried them like Viking treasure-ships and dug them up again in the spring. Jimmy knew this wasn't true. It was just Teddy being funny. By winter the pond was just a pond—half an acre of space surrounded by gaunt trees with the level of the ice about three feet below the pond's edge. Perhaps some of the water had gone underground with the boats, Jimmy thought bitterly.

Then he had his idea. This very instant he

could make a start at being brave ...

The pond's surface stretched away like a frosted window laid flat. He couldn't tell how thick the ice was on top or how deep the water was beneath. But he could try it out. What was it he had to do? That student, Miss Dixon, had taught a lesson on it long ago in October when his own teacher had been away and he'd spent the day in the top class with Teddy and Pete and Kit.

"... Think about it," Miss Dixon said. "What part of you is taking all your weight? Kit?"

"Your feet."

"Right. Now does that mean the weight is pressing down on a big area or a little area?"

"A little area," said Pete.

"Depends on the size of your feet," said Godfrey. "I mean—Jimmy's got little dimity feet but Fatty Rosewell in the secondary school, he's got feet like frying-pans."

Everyone laughed including Miss Dixon.

"That's true," she said. "People's feet do come in different sizes. My own are quite big, you'll notice. But there's never that much difference. The point is that a lot of heaviness on a little bit of space puts on too much pressure. That's what cracks the ice. So what can you do about it?"

"Diet," said Godfrey.

Everyone laughed again. Some kids overdid it a bit which was what Godfrey was after.

"That would take rather a long time," said Miss Dixon briskly, "and it might not work because it's not easy to shrink some parts of your body. Your head, for example."

That shut Godfrey up. Teddy raised his hand.

"What about spreading out your weight?" he suggested. "I mean you can't do much about how heavy you are but you could sort of alter the area it's pressing on."

"How could you do that?" Godfrey demanded.

"Well ... you could go down on your hands and knees."

"That's right," said Pete. "You lie on your feet and slide yourself over the ice."

"Exactly," Miss Dixon agreed. "Smashing, Teddy! Well done, Pete! The important thing is to spread out your weight as much as you can. So if you *do* see someone who's plunged through the ice and is struggling and there's no one else around to help, then *crawl* over the ice until you're close enough to give them something to catch on to—a piece of rope or your coat or the branch of a tree. Okay? Don't try to reach them standing up. You'd just go through the ice yourself. You've got to act fast because a person can't live very long in freezing water. Also the person might be a non-swimmer, of course. But you mustn't hurry it whatever you do."

That was Miss Dixon's advice. And whatever he did Jimmy wasn't going to hurry it. He sat on the stone surround of the pond and touched the ice with his toecap. It seemed firm enough. But that was near the edge. Did it get thicker or thinner at the centre? They'd also talked about that in the lesson but Jimmy couldn't remember

60

what was said. Perhaps he should stay on the outside of the pond this first time ...

No. That would be chicken. He had to cross it. Gingerly, sitting on the pond's edge, he lowered both feet onto the surface. Still firm. Supporting his weight with his hands he shifted to his knees then let go and eased forward ... slowly, slowly ... until he lay full-length stretched out like a starfish. From beneath him came a sound like the crunching of tiny egg shells. But that was just the snow on top of the ice, surely. Perhaps he should leave the next move until tomorrow.

No. That would be chicken too. He slithered forward, shivering at first from fright not cold. For a while he was protected by the thick woollens his Mum insisted he wore ... till wetness began to seep through here-and-there bringing with it a bone-aching chill. Half-sliding, half-crawling and despite Miss Dixon's instructions, he increased his speed. Each second he expected a sudden splitting and a rush of water. And shock. The shock itself could kill you. Some kid in the class had said that. And supposing you got trapped under the ice—coughing and spluttering to death in a frigid darkness? Jimmy whimpered at the thought of it. How far had he got to go? He lifted his head to look and the whimper died away. He had reached the centre of the pond already.

He could hardly believe it. He shifted to look behind him. From the pond's stone rim to where he lay was a trail of disturbed snow, ice-bound underneath. There was no hint of a crack. Miss Dixon had been right. Or was the water frozen so solid that he needn't have been so cautious? After all people did actually *skate* on ice. This ice felt as solid as rock apart from the crunching eggshell sound and he'd got used to that. Maybe ... maybe *he* could stand up like a skater. Did he dare?

With treetops and diving-boards also in mind Jimmy inch-by-inched to his feet. His teeth were gritted, his fists clenched. To his astonishment he found he was sweating. Once, almost there, he slipped. Just in time he recovered his balance. Finally, arms spread like a high-wire walker, he was upright. He wanted to grin, but didn't, in case that was enough to topple him. All he had to do now was settle how he got back— walking or crawling, over new ice or over the ice he'd already tested. He swivelled, trying to decide which, and at the top of the slope something caught his eye.

Far off on the hill's crest three kids were getting a toboggan into position. One straddled the front, one the rear and the third squeezed into the middle. Three boys on one sledge? Crazy, Jimmy thought. Then he saw it was Teddy and Pete and Kit. He saw them using their legs like oars as they propelled the toboggan forward. Once it was on the move they tucked up their knees and hunched their shoulders, urging it faster. Jimmy stared in horror. They were coming straight at him—at the pond! Couldn't they *see*? Surely they'd swerve. They'd stop short ...

"Look out!" Jimmy cried.

On and on came the toboggan.

"Slow down," Jimmy croaked.

At that pace and with that weight and given the three foot drop down to him he knew the sledge would shatter the pond like glass. He could see an explosion of ice on impact with cracks cobwebbing over the whole surface, reaching him even. Would they all be drowned?

"Please!" he bleated.

Still the toboggan came on.

"You'll break it!" he screeched. "You'll break it!" Already it was too late. He saw the toboggan reach a peak of speed at the pool's edge and rocket into the air. In a commotion of snow it clattered onto the pond's surface spilling Teddy and Kit and Pete on either side like a bronco bucking three riders at once.

"You'll break it," Jimmy whispered.

And break it they had. But not the ice. Where the sledge had landed Jimmy saw the concrete base of the pool. A pool empty of water. He still didn't know what the park-keepers did with the boats in winter but he knew what happened to the pond. They drained it.

The toboggan was what had been broken. One runner had snapped completely and the other was bent. The chassis had come apart. Sheepishly Teddy and Pete and Kit got to their feet.

"Maybe ... maybe your dad could sort of repair it," said Pete, brushing himself down.

Teddy shook his head.

"No. We've wrecked it. Have to be re-built completely."

"Couldn't have been very well made," Kit snorted. "I mean it wasn't that much of a crash."

"Shut up," Teddy snapped. "We've wrecked it, that's all. Sorry Jim. I'll tell your dad it was us."

"It doesn't matter," Jimmy said.

To their surprise he wasn't in tears. There was a grin on his face almost.

"I wasn't much good at it anyway," he added.

"All you needed was practice," said Teddy.

"And you won't get any now," said Pete. "Thanks to us."

"Well, we didn't do it on purpose," Kit protested. "Must've been the design of the thing."

"Leave off," grated Teddy. "We wrecked it. Simple as that. We shouldn't all have ridden it together and that was your idea if I remember rightly."

"Forget it," said Jimmy. "It was funny, really."

"Funny?" they echoed.

"In a way."

But he didn't tell them in what way and they didn't ask. They were too relieved to have him smiling about it as he helped them gather up the pieces.

· Mad Eric ·

He spent his time in the park, mostly. So you could almost always see him coming. As a rule he used the west gate, from the main road. Now and again, though, he arrived by the gate to the east. This was when he took you by surprise. Who would expect Mad Eric to appear from a trim avenue of privet and bungalows each with its own garage? Even when he came that way next time you didn't expect it.

The safest place was in the middle of the park. Here there were four widely-spaced oak trees, a paddling pool, a rain shelter, a swing and a roundabout. The rest was just grass. You had more than a hundred yards of it all round you. He hadn't a scrap of cover. After all, even Eric couldn't clamber over the eight foot wall of the graveyard on the third side of the park or crawl under the fence along the railway track that made the fourth. Which meant there were only two directions he could approach from—except, of course in nightmares. Kids would dream of Eric battering through from the cemetery with an uprooted tombstone or leaping onto the swing from the roof of a passing train. In real life, though, it was usually enough to keep an eye on the main road.

He was easily noticed. Only Eric had a walk like that. "Like a puppet," Teddy declared, "like a big puppet. You expect to see a huge hand hovering over his head an' strings coming down." Everyone laughed.

"Don't be nasty. He can't help it," Pete protested.

"Neither can I," said Teddy. "Just look at him."

"What, you can't help it either?" Jimmy giggled. "You mean you're like Eric?"

"I mean I can't help him being like that, stupid."

"That explains it," Kit said.

"Explains what?"

"Explains what you and Eric have in common. You both can't help it. I'm glad you told me that."

"I didn't say that," Teddy snapped. "Pete said he couldn't help it and I"

"What, Pete can't help it either?" interrupted Kit. "That means three of you!"

"It's like an epidermis," spluttered Jimmy.

"Epidemic," Kit corrected. "And there's no cure, either. You've both had it, I'm afraid. Mental for life."

Pete dusted the palms of his hands.

"Teddy," he sighed, "I think it's time we

duffed these two up."

"Hey, that's not fair. You outnumber us two-to-one."

"Two-to-one? How d'you make that out? Teddy and me against you and Jimmy."

"Jimmy only counts as half—he's only eight. And you'll have Eric on your side. All mentals stick together. That makes three against one-and-a-half."

"Get him," Pete said.

"Hey!" shrilled Jimmy. "Eric's coming over here! He's waving!"

The others froze in mid-fight. He certainly seemed to be waving. It was difficult to be sure because Eric's walk was so odd that the jerking of his hand could have been just a new way of keeping his balance.

"What shall we do?" Kit asked.

"See what he wants," said Teddy. "Why, you scared?"

"Course not."

"You look scared."

"Get off! Let's get on with the cricket."

"Let's see what he wants," Teddy insisted. It took a little time. Eric moved in too many directions at once to get anywhere fast. At least this meant you were reminded of his uglinesses one by one.

"That hair," said Pete.

"All smarmed down and the colour of dog what-not," Teddy commented.

"What about his ears?" laughed Jimmy.

"Look like an extra pair of hands stuck on his head," Kit said.

"And his teeth—all jagged and mossy."

"That funny eye that never looks at you."

"The one that does look at you is worse—the way it bulges."

"And those pimples."

"Septic."

"The plague, probably."

"The lurgy."

"The pox."

"The lurgy, definitely."

"He killed an Alsatian once," Jimmy said. "Strangled it."

"Where d'you hear that?" demanded Teddy. Jimmy reddened.

"It's true. My mum told me."

"They get extra strength," said Kit. "All mad people do."

"Eric's not mad," Teddy snorted. "He's just simple." But he looked mad. As he approached they fell silent, even Teddy. He had a jumble-sale suit on and a mac that reached his ankles though it hadn't rained for a fortnight. As usual his nose was running. Kit hated this especially. It was nearly as bad as the cotton wool he always had in his ears. One thing was new though. On his raincoat he'd pinned a spray of dandelions and grass and daisies.

"'Lo, boys," he said.

"Hello Eric."

"Wha you doin'?"

"Playing cricket," said Teddy.

"I kin play cricket."

"Can you?"

"I kin play good cricket."

"Yes? Didn't know that."

"I'm a good cricket player."

"Really?"

"Yeh. Can I 'ave game cricket, boys?"

Jimmy and Kit and Pete looked at Teddy. Surely he wouldn't say yes? Suppose you and Eric went for the same ball and you bumped into him? What if you were batting and he was wicket-keeper? He'd be right in close all the time, behind your back.

"Sure you can," said Teddy at last. Kit nearly goaned. Eric gave a squeal of excitement. He began to make feet-wiping movements on the grass. Warming up, perhaps.

"Providing you've got your licence," Teddy added.

"Wha'?"

"Your Rec. Cricket Licence. You've got one, haven't you?"

"Wha'?"

"Don't tell me you haven't got one, Eric? Good cricketer like you?"

"Na."

"No licence?"

"Na."

Teddy smiled helplessly.

"Sorry, Eric. We'd have our licences taken away if we let you play without one. More than our lives' worth. Pity that. Could've been a good game."

"I'm a good cricket player," said Eric.

" You haven't got a licence, though, have you?"

"Na."

"Sorry Eric," said Teddy.

Eric moved away. He looked more baffled than disappointed. The posy of weeds on his lapel suddenly caught his eye. With a gurgle of delight he turned back. He began to hug himself and jump up and down on the spot. His laugh was like a car's starter-motor misfiring.

"What's the matter with him?" Kit asked.

"Don't know," said Teddy. " What's up Eric?"

"Got a secret!"

"What about? Tell us, Eric."

"Na!"

Eric shook his head hard. He lifted a finger to tap his nose. This meant you were to mind your own business. Only Eric got it wrong and put the finger up his nose.

"Go on Eric," Teddy urged.

"Na!"

"Why not?"

"Secret."

"Look," said Teddy, "if you don't tell us we'll just have to stop asking. We haven't got all day." That persuaded Eric. He glanced over his shoulder one way, then the other. His face broke into a smile. You could see the shadow of his front teeth on his chin. Without closing his mouth he sniffed, coyly, at the dandelions in his buttonhole.

"Goin' get married," he announced.

"Who—you?"

"Yeh."

"When Eric?" Pete asked.

"Next week."

"Who to?"

"Girl."

"Well that helps," said Teddy. "What's her name?"

Eric hesitated.

"She's pretty," he said. "Goin' to marry her. Goin' to buy a ring. Goin' to get married."

"She's pretty," he added.

"Bet she is. Congratulations, Eric."

"Congratulations, Eric," said Pete and Jimmy.

"'Ngratulations," Eric repeated.

Up on the embankment a train clattered past. They turned to look automatically, counting the carriages. Seven was lucky. Its noise drowned Eric's next remark.

"Eight," said Kit, as the sound died away.

"What did you say, Eric?" asked Teddy.

"Want you to be my best man."

"Who—me?"

"When I get married."

"Next week?"

"Yeh."

"Great," said Teddy. "See you at the church."

"She's pretty."

"I'd go and buy that ring, Eric," Teddy suggested. "I've got to have one to hand over when I'm best man. Now if you don't mind I want to get on with this game. My Cricket Licence'll be expiring soon."

"Goin' to get married," said Eric.

Still beaming he set off towards the rain shelter. His walk seemed even odder from behind. He looked as if he were playing copy-cat in a chicken run. No one spoke till he was out of ear-shot.

71

"Married?" exclaimed Pete. "Eric?"

"What kind of girl would marry him?" Jimmy asked.

"Oh, I don't know," grinned Teddy. "There are some pretty peculiar girls around."

"Not that peculiar," said Kit. "Not even a girl can be that peculiar. You don't really think he's going to get married, do you Teddy?"

Teddy shrugged. "He can't live with his mum all his life, can he?"

They knew Eric's mum, a grey-haired, bent little lady. Sometimes she came to the park with him.

"He couldn't even tell us her name!" Kit scoffed.

"Maybe he didn't want to," Pete said. "Maybe he was afraid you might decide you'd rather be the bridegroom than the best man."

"I'll duff *you* up in a minute," said Teddy.

"The way you said about the Cricket Licence," Jimmy chortled. "That was good."

"Stroke of genius," agreed Pete. "I really thought we'd got lumbered with him there."

"Wouldn't have hurt us," Teddy said.

"Eh?"

"Don't suppose he gets much chance to have a game of cricket. Wouldn't be surprised if he'd never played before."

"Well you stopped him playing this time," said Kit.

"I know," said Teddy.

Kit picked up the cricket bat in disgust. Teddy's attitude annoyed him. He was being all holy now, but he hadn't minded the looks of admiration he'd been getting from Jimmy and Pete a moment before. Stroke of genius! Teddy hadn't been that clever.

"I'm batting," he said, sourly.

Kit was still thinking about it as Jimmy came up to bowl. He knew it wasn't true—but just suppose it was? Suppose Eric did get married? Suppose he had children? He had a sudden vision of half-a-dozen little Erics running round the park, all with ankle-length macs and cotton wool in their ears. And all getting bigger and madder every day ...

"Howzat!" screamed Teddy and Jimmy and Pete. Kit looked behind him in surprise. His off-stump lay flat on the ground.

"Wasn't ready," he protested.

"Rubbish," said Pete. "My turn. You're fielding. Great ball, Jimmy."

"He didn't even see it," Jimmy crowed.

"I wasn't ready!"

"Come on Kit," said Teddy. "Don't be a lousy sport."

Kit handed the bat over. Biting his lips, he stalked to his fielding position. Eric again, he thought bitterly. Now he'd got him bowled, first ball, by an eight-year-old. It would be ages before his turn to bat came round again. Moodily he kicked at a clump of turf. They needn't expect him to strain himself fielding. Let Jimmy do his own chasing.

From where he'd placed himself, he could hardly hear the others. Not that they were taking any notice. The ball came nowhere near him. He wasn't even able to take his time about returning it. Perhaps they thought he was sulking, or something. Kit gave a heavy sigh at the injustice of it all.

"Got it!" said Eric. "Look."

Kit snapped upright and swung round. Eric was so close you could have wiped his nose for him. He was holding a scrap of paper. Kit took a step backwards.

"What's that?" he croaked, when he'd found his voice.

"My Licen'. For the cricket."

Kit stared at it blankly.

"Where d'you get it?" he asked.

Eric's face went crafty. He shook his head.

"Let's see it, Eric."

"My Licen'," he said. "Wannit back."

"Only want to see it," said Kit.

He was surprised at his own bravery. When Eric handed the paper over there could only have been a couple of inches between their two hands. Even Teddy hadn't been that near. Kit glanced at the licence. It was written in pencil. It began: five pounds of King Edwards, six tomatoes, two pounds of brussel sprouts ...

"This isn't a licence!" he exclaimed.

"Wa?" asked Eric.

"This is a shopping—"

Kit broke off. His brain reeled. Maybe it *was* a licence. Maybe Teddy wasn't the only one who had strokes of genius ...

"This *is* a licence," he heard himself saying. "You're quite right, Eric. But it isn't a Cricket Licence."

"Na? Wha' is it then?"

"It's a Marriage Licence."

"Wha?"

"It lets you get married. They must have given you the wrong one. Where did you get it?"

Eric blinked. He couldn't believe it. "Found it," he said.

"Found it? And you're getting married next week? That's a bit of luck!"

"Bi' of luck!" said Eric, happily.

"It says here there are strict rules, though. You've got to keep them or you can't get married."

"Huh?"

Kit took a deep breath. His voice had to be as matter of fact as he could make it.

"It says you've got to prove you're ready to get married, Eric. Otherwise it's not fair on the girl. You've got to prove you really love her."

"Wha?"

"You've got to give up some things to show you're serious. Not do them any more. Are you willing to do that, Eric? So you can marry her?" Eric nodded uncertainly. "Yeah," he said. "Wha' go' give up?"

"Well ... some of your pocket-money. You've got to save up for furniture and stuff ... And you've got to agree not to waste your time by coming to parks, like this one."

"Wha?" said Eric.

"You've got to stay right away from here. Only if you're serious about getting married, Eric."

"Wha?" said Eric. "Not come to park no more?"

"That's what it says."

Kit shrugged and held out the scrap of paper. Eric took it. He peered at it, scratching his head. His eyes squinted and his mouth hung open. He turned it sideways, upside-down, then looked at the back.

"No park?" he asked again. "No any more?"

"You could always give your girl up—not get married. You could keep coming then."

To Kit's relief, Eric shook his head.

"Goin' to get married," he insisted, miserably.

"You'll have to obey the rules then," said Kit. Of course, it wouldn't work forever. As soon as he was tired of this marriage game Eric would come back. He'd stay away for a while, though. Maybe even for the rest of the summer holidays. Kit was bursting to tell the others—Teddy, especially. Getting Eric out of your cricket match was one thing. Getting him out of the park altogether was something else: Eric practically lived there. It seemed to Kit he deserved a medal. All the kids who used the park and were afraid of Eric, which meant everybody, ought to club together and buy him one. They could present it to him over by the roundabout. He'd stand on the swing and make a speech. Tell them how he'd done it. Kit's eyes glazed over as he imagined the scene. The corners of his mouth twitched.

Eric's grunt of anger brought him into sharp focus again. Kit straightened his face, hastily. He was too late. Eric's jaw clamped shut. His lips curled back from his teeth.

"You don' believe me," he snarled.

"I do, Eric, I do!" Kit yelped.

"You don' believe me. You making a laugh at me."

"I'm not Eric—honest!"

Eric pawed at the ground with his feet. A noise like a clashing of gears came from his throat. Kit gazed at him in horror, not moving. Clawing at the air, Eric lurched forward. The shreds of the marriage licence fluttered down to the grass. Still Kit didn't move. Not until Eric's bony fist had smacked down on the top of his head did Kit run. Then he ran.

"Help! Help! Eric's gone mad!" he shrieked. By the time he passed the cricket match, full pelt, the others were already in motion. They were almost level with him at the park gates, despite carrying the equipment. Halfway along the avenue, they finally slowed to a trot.

"It's all right," Teddy gasped. "He's not following any more."

"You sure?" spluttered Pete.

"He didn't even leave the park. He fell over twice—got his foot caught in the lining of his raincoat."

They halted, clutching their sides and fighting for breath.

"What made him go like that?' Teddy asked.

"They have fits," said Jimmy. "That's when they strangle Alsatians."

"What set him off, though?"

All three looked at Kit. He was wiping the sweat from his face with a shirt-sleeve. They didn't catch his answer.

"What?" Pete demanded.

"Nothing."

"Must've been something," said Teddy. "He didn't just attack you from behind, did he?"

"No."

"Well, what then?"

Kit stared back towards the park gates, his cheeks flushed. He couldn't see Eric.

"He showed me a piece of paper. An old shopping list. Said it was a Cricket Licence."

"Cunning old thing!" Teddy whistled. "What did you do—tell him it wasn"t?"

"Yes. He hit me on the head."

"You should have agreed with him."

"Oh great!" said Pete. "And let him lose his temper later on with a cricket bat in his hand? Wipe us all out."

"Suppose so," Teddy admitted.

"You're just disappointed because you won't be best-man any more," giggled Jimmy.

"Old Eric'll probably hit the vicar with a pew!" laughed Pete.

"—And eat his prayer book!" Jimmy suggested.

"And blow bubbles with the organ-pipes," added Teddy.

All the way home they did impressions of Eric's wedding or of Eric getting his foot caught in his raincoat, or of Eric playing cricket. Except Kit, who didn't join in. This was because he was feeling the effects of being hit on the head, perhaps.

· Thingy ·

Once upon a time there wasn't a Thingy—not
really. Thingy was what you called someone
whose name you couldn't remember. You'd say
something like "Hey ... er ... Thingy ... bring
over the pencil-sharpener, would you?" Or
some kid would say to you "Here, guess who
we saw in the park last Saturday. Old ... um
... Thingy—you know who I mean." Somehow
you did know, usually.

But then the name Thingy got attached to
just one person—to Lorna Penfold. Lorna
Penfold became the one and only Thingy.
After that if you called anyone else Thingy
they bashed you up. If they were big enough,
that is. If they weren't then they'd scowl and
they'd say "yuk" and they'd pretend to brush
something messy off their sleeve. No one
wanted to be called the same name as Lorna
Penfold.

Even the boys talked about her.

"Heard the latest?" someone would say.

"What about?"

"Thingy."

"No? What's up?"

"Well—it's about her Dad, really. Old man Penfold. He's in prison again. Got taken away last week."

"What for?"

"Don't know. But it's definitely true. My mum knows someone who knows the welfare-worker. Says they're having to clean the house from top to bottom.'"

"Why?"

"Dog's muck."

"Dog's muck?"

"Dog's muck. From his greyhounds. They had the run of the house, they reckon. Never got let out. All the assistance money went on feeding them. Welfare-worker's getting rid of them. Thingy's Dad'll go mad when he gets back."

Some of the gossip about Thingy you could only whisper, though. About her mum, for example. And another subject nobody liked to discuss out loud was how Thingy came to have only one-and-a-half arms instead of two.

This was the first thing other kids noticed. Her tattered clothes and her smelliness only came later. Just about where her elbow should have been, Thingy's right arm ended in a flap of skin like a balloon not fully blown up. Everyone hated the sight of it. It was strange when, for a while, Thingy's stump made her the most important person in the playground.

This happened in the Spring term. The air

was still sharp but there were smudges of green in the churchyard trees next door and it was the time for gangs. Every kid had to be in a gang. And to get in a gang you had to do the membership tests set by the gang-leader. You had to run fast enough or jump high enough or do something daring. All the time you saw the kids being tested.

Only one gang-leader so far had refused to name the test for his gang. He was the biggest, most important leader of all—Raymond Essex. After four days the other big and important boys were tired of being kept waiting.

"Hey, Raymond," Teddy said. "Is it today?"

"Might be."

"Come on, Raymond," said Pete. "All the other gangs are already formed, practically."

"Maybe we should join one of them," said Kit bitterly. "Or start one of our own."

"Go ahead," said Raymond.

That shut Kit up. Aloofly, Raymond scanned the playground. On the fringe of a group of smaller boys was Thingy. She always preferred the boys to leave her out than the girls.

"Hey, Thingy!" shouted Raymond. Thingy turned. When she saw who was calling her mouth gaped open in surprise.

"Come over here!" Raymond beckoned. The big and most important boys looked at each other, pulling faces. Thingy trotted over.

"Want to help with the tests for my gang, Thingy?" Raymond asked.

"What?"

"You don't have to," said Raymond.

"Yes I will," blurted Thingy.

"You sure?"

Thingy nodded warily.

"Right," said Raymond. "All-y, All-y in those who want to be in my gang."

"All-y, All-y in!" whooped the others. Even kids who already belonged to gangs, or who knew they wouldn't stand a chance, gathered round. Raymond's tests were always worth watching.

"Okay," said Raymond. "There's only one thing you've got to do if you want to get in my gang. Who wants to try it?"

A circle of hands shot up. He glanced at Thingy again.

"Sure you want to help?" he asked.

"Course," said Thingy.

The corner of Raymond's mouth twitched.

"Here we go, then—the membership test for my gang. All you've got to do is this. See Thingy's stump?"

Everyone looked. Thingy lifted it uncertainly.

"You've got to kiss it," said Raymond. Several kids gasped. All round, the raised hands wilted. Some dropped altogether. Thingy's face was stiff as a mask. Beneath her lank hair her eyes glinted. No one spoke. Raymond's grin was half a sneer and half a giggle.

"Nobody fancy it?" he asked. "Well that's that, then. Sorry, Thingy. They don't seem to want to kiss your stump. I'll just have to think up some easier test for next week—maybe. All-y, All-y out, then."

"Just a minute," Teddy said.

Those who'd already begun to move off, stopped. Something about Teddy's voice held them.

"You got something to say?" Raymond asked.

"Sure," said Teddy. "You serious that's the test for your gang?"

"Just said it, didn't I?"

"And you're not going to back down on it?"

"Me?" said Raymond. "I'm not doing any backing down. Thought you lot had done that."

"No we haven't," said Teddy. "Just couldn't believe it was so simple to get in your gang, that's all."

He stepped forward.

"Okay, Thingy?"

Quickly he bent and kissed her stump. When he straightened his face was expressionless.

"There," he shrugged. "Really tough that was. Anyone else want to join Raymond's gang?" There was a pause while the kids looked at each other.

"I will," said Pete.

"I will," Kit echoed. Most of the bigger and more important boys called out then. They edged forward one after the other. Some of them made a face when it came to their turn or rubbed their mouth afterwards in a funny way. Others treated it like Teddy. Soon all the kids you'd expect to be in Raymond's gang had joined.

"That's the lot," snapped Raymond. "No more. All-y, all-y out."

"Wait a minute," Jimmy protested. "I'm next in line. I want to take the test."

Raymond scowled and shook his head.

"No little kids. You're only eight."

"What's that matter? It's if you can do the test—that's what counts. Isn't that right, Teddy?"

"That's right," said Teddy.

"If we let him join they'll all join," Raymond snorted. "We won't be a gang, we'll be a bunch of—of babysitters!"

"Can't help that," Teddy said. "You set the test. Told you it was too simple. Mind you, there is one way you could keep the shrimps out without backing down."

"How's that?"

"Well ... *you* can't stop people taking the test. That's not fair. But Thingy could. All she's got to do is not to let anyone else kiss her stump. And you could make sure of that quite easily."

"How?"

"Let Thingy join the gang. She wouldn't muck up her own gang, would she?"

"What!" Raymond yelped.

"How can you stop her?" Teddy pointed out. "She's only got to kiss her own stump and she's joined. Want to be in the gang, Thingy?"

Thingy's fixed look had slipped. She couldn't believe it.

"Yes," she said.

"Well, kiss your stump then and you're in." Still staring at Teddy, Thingy brushed her arm with her lips. In the crowd someone sniggered.

"That," Raymond grated, "just about puts the tin lid on it."

"No it doesn't," said Teddy. "What about you?"

"Me?"

"Your turn. You haven't done the test yourself yet."

"Me?"

"You," Teddy insisted. Raymond swallowed. "I don't get it. What's the matter with you? What you sticking up for her for? You in love with her or something? Hey, get this you lot! Teddy Beckenham's got a crush on Thingy! When you going to marry him, Thingy?"

"When you going to take the test?" asked Teddy, coolly. "Or are you scared to kiss Thingy's stump?" Standing on either side of him, Kit and Pete felt Teddy trembling. You'd never guess this from the way he looked, though. Next to Godfrey Fanshaw he always had been the best actor in the school.

"I'm not scared," said Raymond. "But I'm not going to take the test either."

"You've got to," shrugged Teddy. "Gang-leader's got to show he can do his own test."

"Not this one," said Raymond.

"You can't be leader, then. Come to that you can't even be in the gang."

"That so? Mind telling me who *is* leader of the gang, then? You maybe?"

"I was first," said Teddy. "Reckon I must be."

"Reckon you must be," repeated Raymond. "Reckon you're a good enough fighter to be

leader of the gang?"

"Don't know."

"Reckon you'd like to find out? After school say?" Teddy's chin trembled.

"Okay," he said.

"That ain't fair—that ain't fair!" Thingy burst out. "You can murder him!"

"Your girlfriend thinks it's not fair," said Raymond. "Do you think it's fair?"

"Course," said Teddy. "She's not my girl-friend," he added.

"No? Funny—thought she was. After school, then. And no chanting."

"No chanting," Teddy agreed.

"That ain't fair!" Thingy screamed. "That ain't fair!"

In a way she was right. Without chanting Teddy hadn't a hope. When the kids yelled "Fight! Fight! Fight!" a teacher came running. It was a way of making sure no one got badly hurt. With silent watchers, though, it could easily be ten minutes before a grown-up realized what was happening. It was a point of honour that the fight went on till then. And ten minutes was more than enough for Raymond. He was the most vicious fighter in the district.

All afternoon Teddy had to put up with kids who smiled wryly and asked him what flowers he wanted. Worse, he had to put up with Thingy who didn't take her eyes off him.

By five past four the playground was ready. Using the netball-markings, the kids had formed an arena. Those in the front had linked hands. In the centre were Raymond and Teddy. The silence was eerie. A few of the younger kids had started by calling "All-y, all-y in" but they were soon shut up. There was to be no chanting. Teddy had agreed to it.

"Okay?" asked Raymond.

"Okay."

Both boys edged apart a pace or two. They bunched their fists and dropped into a half-crouch. Somewhere at the back Thingy gave a howl of misery.

"That your girlfriend?" Raymond enquired. Teddy swung with everything he'd got. The punch caught Raymond square on the chin. He staggered and nearly fell. Then he straightened up.

"That the best you can do?" he asked.

"Fraid so," said Teddy.

"Well here's my second-best," said Raymond. He lashed out. Teddy's head seemed to jerk almost from his neck. Five or six more blows followed until Teddy crumpled. Sucking a tooth, Raymond waited for him to get up. One of Teddy's eyes was already closed and blood smeared his nose and mouth. He got to his feet slowly. At once everyone gasped. Through thick lips Teddy was whistling—actually whistling. Casually, he tossed the hair from his eyes. With dainty flicks he dusted himself down.

"Okay, fatso," he said. "Your knuckles have had it. My face is going to smash them to pieces."

"I see—a funny man," Raymond snarled. Again he let fly, both fists thudding home. There was no way Teddy could dodge. His attempts to hit back were brushed aside. Down he went again. Some kids had turned away, unable to bear it. It was some while before Teddy got up this time. When he did ... he blew Raymond a kiss. Raymond stared in disbelief. Then he kicked savagely, catching Teddy on the shin. Teddy gasped.

"Naughty, naughty!" he said. "Lickle Donkey!" Suddenly everyone could see what Teddy was trying to do. The more he was cut to pieces the more he was going to clown.

"You won't be making a joke of it for long," Raymond spat.

He didn't sound convinced, though. Already it might be too late. People had actually started laughing. Laughing! What if Teddy were carried off on a stretcher, still cocky? What if the littlest kids in the school were to copy Teddy's tactics? Uneasily Raymond lifted his fists. Teddy was jabbing the air with his like an old-time prize-fighter. He gave his opponent a huge wink. Raymond moved forward. But now, in a strange way, he looked as if he were going backwards.

Suddenly, a voice had the playground stock-still.

"You two boys stop that! This very second!"

It was old Miss Manly. She stood in the school doorway next to Thingy. No one had seen Thingy slip away.

"Thank you, Lorna," Miss Manly said. " You've been very sensible. You two boys come to my room. The rest of you get off home—this instant!"

Miss Manly stalked into school. She never

had to wait to see if she was obeyed. The first kids were already moving towards the gate. As they passed Thingy they hissed under their breath and bared their teeth and made clawing movements with their hands.

"Very sensible, your girlfriend," Raymond remarked.

At the door Thingy tried to explain.

"You'd a got murdered," she said.

Teddy's swollen face was twisted with anger. He could hardly get the words out.

"You idiot! You stupid, stupid stinking idiot!" The door slammed behind him. Thingy blinked. For a while she stood there staring at the woodwork. Then she turned for the other gate, into the churchyard. It was the long way round but she knew that if you ran and were lucky you could get home without meeting any big and important kids. If you were lucky you could get home without meeting any kids at all.

• Jesus Wants Me for a Comrade •

If someone were to ask you about the wickedest thing you ever did, what would you say? I know what I would say—at least I know what I would say if I had the guts. But probably I'd keep quiet. You see, the wickedest thing I ever did happened by mistake. It got me thrown out of Sunday-school nearly.

Godfrey Fanshaw started it.

"See that girl," he remarked, with a jerk of his head.

My brother Pete and I looked across the road, casually. She was just a girl, about our age, walking along with a shopping basket. There didn't seem anything special about her.

"Yes?" said Pete.

He yawned as he said it. It was fatal to let Godfrey see you were interested. He was enough of a bighead already.

"I know something about her father," Godfrey said.

"What about him?" I asked.

"He's a Communist." We nodded and raised our eyebrows in a really-how-interesting kind of way. The trouble was we really were interested. We'd come across the word "Communist" before, naturally. But neither of us had any idea what it meant. Except that it was definitely wrong to be one. The problem was to get Godfrey to explain without letting on we didn't already know.

"A Communist?" I repeated.

"So they tell me," said Godfrey.

He made it sound as if "they" were the Prime Minister and the Archbishop of Canterbury. He was like that. A personal friend of the Royal Family Godfrey was.

"Didn't know they were allowed in this country," said Pete.

"Must be. He's one."

"What—the same as abroad?" I asked cunningly.

"Huh?"

"English ones are different, aren't they?" Godfrey shook his head.

"Same everywhere," he said, "Communists."

We watched the girl as she passed. She looked fantastically ordinary for someone whose dad was a Communist. There was something sinister about it. They'd probably trained her for years to look the same as everybody else.

"My dad says they're taking over the whole country," said Godfrey. "Them and the Jews."

"Hey!" Pete exclaimed. "She's going in a house." The girl had turned into a side-alley right opposite where we lived.

"She knows someone in your road, then," said Godfrey.

The way he said it condemned the whole street. Straight away the houses looked smaller and older and uglier. What little colour there was in the February afternoon seemed to drain away.

"Nice," Godfrey sniffed, "having Communists for neighbours."

"Get off!" I snapped. "She's not a neighbour. She's just visiting."

"Same thing."

"Same thing?" I echoed. "How d'you make that out? That'd mean the milkman was a neighbour and the rent man and the man who collects the insurance. And they all live miles away. Suppose they're all Communists, too."

"Or their fathers," added Pete.

Godfrey shrugged.

"Wouldn't know what happens round here."

"Don't suppose you would," I snorted. "Don't suppose you even know what a Communist *is*." Godfrey snapped upright. He scowled and thrust out a hand.

"Wanna bet?"

"Bet."

We shook on it fiercely.

"What's a Communist, then?" I demanded.

"It's someone who doesn't believe in God, see!"

"What?" I yelped.

"Communists don't believe in God. That's what a Communist is, Mr Clever-Clogs."

"What—not at all?" I gasped.

"Course they don't," said Godfrey.

He looked at me suspiciously.

"Didn't you know that?"

"I was thinking of the foreign version," I said hastily.

"They're no different," said Godfrey. "Communists are the same all over my dad says. They don't believe in God or Jesus or the Bible or Heaven or Hell or anything."

I still couldn't take it in.

"Who do they think made the world, then?" I asked faintly. "Who do they think started it all off?"

Godfrey didn't know that. In fact he didn't seem to know much more than he'd said already. So he swanked for a few minutes longer then he went home. Pete and I stared across the street.

" Course he can't blame us," I said. " Can he?"

"Who?" Pete asked.

"God."

"Blame us for what?"

"For them. For the Communists. Living over the road and that."

"Course not," scoffed Pete.

That was the trouble with Pete. He always left the worrying to me. And if Godfrey Fanshaw was right about the girl and about Communists then I had plenty to worry about.

Partly I was worried about the effect on God. After all, you couldn't have people not believing in you. I knew how I'd feel if people didn't believe in me. In the end, if they kept it up, you'd probably go mad. The thought of God going a bit mental, like Mad Eric, terrified me. At bedtime I mentioned the Communists in my prayers in case God hadn't realized the danger. This was the other reason I was worried about the Communists opposite: would they distract God's attention from answering prayers? I had a prayer I expected to be answered any day now. It would make my dad a rich man. I was very keen on my dad getting rich.

To begin with I'd nearly ruined everything by praying for a lot of money straight out. I could see now why this might not be a good approach. At Sunday-school, Mr Penny had been quite firm about it.

"When the young man came to Jesus," Mr Penny declared, "and asked him what he should do to be saved, Jesus told him that being good wasn't enough. He had to give up everything he had and become a disciple. What did the young man do then? Kit?"

"He was fed up. He went away," I replied.

"Why was that, Pete?"

"He was loaded. He wanted to keep his money."

"Correct," said Mr Penny. "Remember what it says in the Bible, boys. It is better to give than to receive. It's easier for a camel to pass through the eye of a needle than for a rich man to enter the Kingdom of Heaven." David Clifford gave a shy cough.

"I don't get it," he said.

"What's that, David?"

"I don't see how that can be true. Who was he supposed to give his money to?"

"To the poor, you prune," said Teddy scornfully.

"But that would make them rich. Then *they* couldn't get into Heaven."

"Ah," said Mr Penny. "But he could give a lot of people a small amount. Not enough to make them rich."

David Clifford shook his head. He was blinking nervously. In the bare whiteness of the chapel he always looked his weediest.

"But if *they* are supposed to give up everything and become disciples then who do *they* give it to?" he asked.

"And it's better to give than to receive," agreed Teddy, catching on. "You said that."

"Ah ..." said Mr Penny.

We all perked up.

"Somebody's bound to get lumbered with it in the end," Pete said.

"The last one could bury it," I suggested, "like treasure."

"Need a big hole," said Teddy.

"Need the Grand Canyon," said Pete.

"Need Godfrey Fanshaw," I said.

"With his mouth he could swallow it!" We all laughed—except Mr Penny and David Clifford, who was still looking puzzled.

"He can't bury it," he objected. "That's what the man did last week. You know, Mr Penny—what was it called? The Parable of the Talents or something."

"I remember," Teddy grinned. "He got given some money along with two other blokes while his boss went abroad. The other two

96

made a profit and he didn't so when his boss came back he duffed him up."

"He did *not*," said Mr Penny.

"Well his boss wasn't too thrilled with him, was he."

"Wonder who they gave it to," said Pete. "The other ones, I mean."

"Maybe *they* buried it," I suggested. "Only afterwards. When the boss wasn't looking."

"They couldn't have," said David Clifford. "Their boss could see everything. Mr Penny said he stood for God, don't you remember?"

"Quite right," said Mr Penny, quickly. "They gave their money—their talents, that is—back to God. Where it belongs. That's the whole point of the story."

"Only after they'd made a pile, though," Pete said. "Can't see why he gave it to them in the first place. Just meant there was all the more to get rid of."

"For the last person to be stuck with," I added. "When everyone else is saved." Mr Penny smiled stiffly.

"The last person—the one who got stuck with it as you put it—would just have to return it to God. Then he would be saved, too."

"But that would make God richest of all," David Clifford pointed out. "So then he couldn't get into Heaven himself."

"Creepers!" said Teddy. "Where would he go? The other place?"

"Certainly not!" snapped Mr Penny. "It doesn't apply to God. God made it all to begin with."

"Oh, I see," sniffed Pete. "He's the exception, is he? That's nice."

"But he didn't make it *all* to begin with," I insisted. "What about the extra money the two men made when he was abroad—when the first one buried his share? If it was God's *already* then the story's daft."

"Who'd want to thread a needle with a camel, anyway?" Teddy asked. "Sounds a bit mental to me."

We went on arguing for a while. Eventually Mr Penny lost his temper and shut us up. For the rest of the group-period we had to do some crayoning. I didn't mind at all. It gave me a chance to practice my drawing for the blackboard. Every week, after group-period, we moved all the chairs back into line and I had to go up to the front and illustrate the afternoon's story while Mr Porter, the Superintendent, told us what we could learn from it. My pictures tended to look alike—all palm-trees and flowing-robes—but that didn't matter. Very bold and tasteful, Mr Porter said. After I'd finished, everyone gave me a clap. It was the best part of Sunday-school. To tell you the truth it was the only part of Sunday-school I really liked.

I thought about the Parable of the Talents for some time after that. There seemed to be two sides to the question, definitely, no matter what Mr Penny said. Perhaps by now, though, God had made up his mind whether money was a good thing or a bad thing. How could I tell which? To be on the safe side I decided to change my prayers. I'd ask God to fix up my dad with a knighthood instead.

This struck me as pretty crafty. In the first place it was for someone else not *me*. Secondly, it didn't even mention money. Yet whoever heard of anyone being called Sir Somebody or other who was poor? The Queen would never allow it. So this way not only did we get to be rich, we got to be posh too. Dad would be Sir Leonard Rowley, Mum would be Lady Rowley and Pete and I would be Right Hons or something. Godfrey Fanshaw would be furious.

Unless, of course, the arrival of the Communists opposite had mucked things up. I could hardly bear to think about it. All that wasted praying—three weeks of it! God couldn't possibly be mingy, could he? Still, I'd better not take any chances. At the next meeting of Sunday-school I'd make sure I was especially well-behaved. I wouldn't argue with Mr Penny. I wouldn't imitate the ups-and-downs of Mr Porter's voice when we sang the hymns. I wouldn't even try to make Teddy giggle during the prayers. And I'd make my picture on the blackboard the best I'd ever done.

Sunday was one of those sharp, bright days that always remind me of Christmas. It was so dazzling inside the chapel that there seemed to be more windows than brickwork. Pete and I took our places next to Teddy and David Clifford in the second row. I was trying so hard to be good we were halfway through the first hymn before I noticed there was someone new at the end of the row in front. She was staring in front of her, not taking her eyes off Mr Porter. It was the girl with the shopping basket—the Communist's daughter.

I nearly fell over from the shock of it. Somehow I stayed on my feet until the hymn finished. All through the notices and the next hymn I struggled to work it out, my mind reeling. Could Godfrey have been wrong about her father? Had she run away because of him, maybe? Had the truth about God dawned on Communists at last? Or was it some kind of plot?

The last thought stunned me. It was so evil and simple. All she had to do each week was to work a few more Communist ideas into the group discussion, slowly getting more and more kids round to her way of thinking. Her father was probably up at the Parish church doing the same thing. Bit by bit the Communists would take over. God would go completely bonkers from not being believed in. Or he'd be forced to wipe out everything with fire, flood and brimstone so he could start all over again. Either way I didn't much fancy it. Mr Porter had to be told at once. I took a step forward, then stopped short. She would deny it all, of course. I could see her doing it. "Me a Communist, Mr Porter? No, Mr Porter. What's a Communist, Mr Porter?" I gritted my teeth with fury.

"Are you all right, Kit?" asked Mr Penny.

"What? Yes—yes, of course," I mumbled.

"Get back in line then, please."

I stepped back. I didn't know what to do.

And why was God letting them get away with it anyway? Couldn't he do something? Then I remembered Dad's favourite religious saying—the shoplifter's motto he called it: "God helps them who help themselves". Perhaps God was waiting for me to make a move.

Group-period was next. We got the chairs in a huddle so Mr Penny could read us the afternoon's story. I tried hard to listen—maybe God would use it to send me a sign.

If He did then I missed it. It was the story of a wedding-feast in Canaan and how Jesus had turned some water into wine after they'd run out. It wasn't a bit of help. When we started to discuss it I kept quiet. I had enough to think about already. My silence was soon noticed.

"Are you sure you're all right, Kit?" Mr Penny asked.

"I'm okay," I said. "Got a headache, that's all."

"Probably the sun," said Mr Penny.

Soon they were too busy arguing to notice me. Mr Penny kept talking about miracles but Teddy claimed he knew how Jesus had done it. He offered to show the whole Sunday-school next week. If Mr Penny would bring the wine, he'd supply his own water.

We ended up crayoning again. This suited me even more than usual. I had to work out a way of stopping the Communists. What infuriated me was that they could send a spy to get at us Christians, but we couldn't send one back ... could we? Or could we? Why not tit-for-tat? All I had to do was to convince her that I was a Communist too and I'd get to know all *their* secrets ... maybe even persuade them about God! It was a brilliant idea! But how was I going to convince her? It wouldn't be enough just to *tell* her. Spying wasn't that easy. She'd want some kind of proof. After all two Communists in one Sunday-school wasn't exactly *likely*. Gloomily I picked up a crayon to finish off my picture of Jesus at the Wedding. As I drew, a plan took shape in my mind. It was so simple it couldn't go wrong and so spectacular she'd have to believe me. My only doubt was whether I'd be brave enough to do it. Just thinking about it made me shiver.

By the time we'd straightened the chairs into rows again I still wasn't sure I'd have the nerve. Mr Porter beckoned me to the front.

"Come on, Kit," he said with a smile. "Let's have our resident artist doing his job."

I didn't feel like an artist. I didn't feel like a spy, either. Standing in front of the blackboard with the chalk in my hand I felt sick. I knew now why heroes got Victoria Crosses. Maybe I'd get one myself. Or a knighthood, even. Maybe they'd do dad and me at the same time. I licked my lips and started to draw while Mr Porter talked.

I began with the usual palm-trees and flat-topped houses. After that came the disciples and the wedding guests, all in flowing robes. Most of the blackboard was taken up with Jesus, of course. Eventually one or two kids in the front row noticed what I was doing. I heard their chairs creak as they nudged each other. Someone in the back row giggled. The whole chapel was looking at my drawing now, except for Mr Porter. He sounded puzzled and annoyed. I moved to one side so that I'd be in the way if he looked around. Having already gone this far I didn't want to be stopped before I was finished. This meant more of the picture could be seen though. It set up a flurry of giggles and whispering which the teachers tried to hush. I heard Teddy laugh out loud. Mr Porter speeded up his summary. I speeded up too. We finished in a dead-heat.

"And now if Kit will stand aside," Mr Porter said, "we'll see what he's produced for us this week. Very bold and ..."

His voice trailed away. Kids were craning round each other for the best view. According to my drawing the wedding-feast in Canaan had been very merry indeed. Especially for Jesus. His halo was on a slant. His hair was a mess. His robe had slipped from one shoulder. He was tilting a bottle, unmistakably marked with three crosses, into a mouth that gaped open beneath a glowing nose. A disciple was holding him up. Everyone else in the picture was clearly as drunk as our Lord.

The chapel was so silent you could have heard the blink of an eye. Then someone started to clap—Teddy probably. After that there was uproar. Mr Porter bent towards me. There was a nasty look on his face.

"Just what do you think *that* is in aid of?" he grated.

"I've decided to turn Communist," I croaked.

"What?"

Mr Porter didn't seem to understand.

"See me afterwards," he hissed. "Now rub out that—that *thing* and go back to your place." All through the closing hymn and the final prayer I held myself poised. I had to move fast now to put the second part of my plan into operation. I was furious with Teddy or whoever had started the clapping. It had drowned my explanation to Mr Porter. Even in the front row she wouldn't have heard it. The instant we all said "Amen" I was off, quick as a whippet. I heard someone call my name as the main door of the chapel clanged shut behind me.

Opposite the Methodist Hall were some car showrooms with a tall elm to one side of the forecourt. I was across the road and behind the tree before any of the other kids were out of the building. If I was careful I could watch the entrance without being seen. Pete and Teddy and David Clifford were almost the last to leave. They were talking loudly.

"Why did he do it?" Teddy exclaimed.

"And where's he gone?" said Pete, looking round.

"Siberia," Teddy said. "That's where I'd be heading. Did you see Mr Porter's face. He was *white*."

"Livid," said David Clifford. "D'you reckon he will go round and see your dad, Pete?"

"Dunno," Pete replied. "Good thing Mr Penny told him that Kit hadn't been well all

104

afternoon. That's the last blackboard drawing Kit'll ever do."

"Creepers!" said Teddy. "Imagine what he'd do with the Last Supper!"

"Or Salome," said David Clifford.

"Salome?" Teddy asked.

"She did this dance. It's in the Bible. The dance of the seven veils."

"What's that?"

"Well ... you couldn't draw it on the blackboard. Not even Kit."

"Why not?"

"Tell us," Pete demanded.

Their voices died away. Almost at once the Communist's daughter appeared—the last kid of all. She crossed the road and walked right past my tree. I stepped from behind the trunk forcing a big grin on my face.

"Hello," I said.

"Hello," she said in surprise. "Aren't you— aren't you the boy who did that picture? In Sunday-school."

"Yes," I said. "I do them every week."

"What—like that?"

"Not always like that," I admitted. "I've only just become a Communist." She looked puzzled.

"A Communist," I repeated. "Like you. Like your dad."

"How did you know that?"

"I get around," I said, airily.

Suddenly she burst out laughing.

"What's the matter?" I asked.

"Your picture," she giggled. "I just thought

of it again. It really was funny. Whatever made you draw it?"

It was the last question I expected from her. I stared at her blankly.

"Why didn't you just tell them you were fed up with doing it?" she went on. "They could easily find someone else. I mean they did, didn't they. They found me."

"You?"

"My group leader suggested me. She showed Mr Porter my crayoning afterwards. That's why I was late coming out. I take over the blackboard picture next week. I like drawing with chalks."

My mouth gaped as wide as Jesus's in my picture. They didn't seem to miss a chance these Communists. Poor Mr Porter. If only he knew what was coming up next week—maybe Salome's dance of the seven veils, whatever that was.

"Should be quite something next Sunday," I said ruefully. "Your first picture in front of everyone. And your last!"

"Why should it be my last?"

"Won't it?" I said. "Won't it be something like mine then?"

"Goodness no! I wouldn't dare! Why should it be?"

"Well, you are a Communist, aren't you?"

"What's that got to do with it?"

I sighed patiently.

"You don't believe in God, then, do you," I pointed out. "That's what makes a Communist a Communist."

She sniffed and tossed her blonde hair.

"It is *not!*" she declared.

I stopped in my tracks.

"It isn't?"

"Of course it isn't. Who told you that? *Some* Communists don't believe in God. Others are very good Christians."

"They are?'

"Yes. Why, my dad says Jesus himself was probably the first Communist. It's not God that Communists don't believe in."

"What don't they believe in then?" I asked faintly.

"Money. Titles and things. You know, Kings and Queens, Lords and Ladies"

"Knighthoods," I suggested in a whisper.

"Yes, Knighthoods," she agreed. "Dad says that God couldn't possibly be in favour of that sort of thing. Dad says you've got to take from everybody according to their ability and give to everybody according to their need. Like in the Parable of the Talents. You know the one where"

"I know it," I managed to say. "We've done it at Sunday-school." She peered at me closely.

"Are you okay?" she asked. "You look a bit seedy."

I mumbled goodbye and turned away. I felt as if my stomach had melted and was sliding down the inside of my legs towards my feet. I staggered home in a daze. Halfway there I threw back my head and let out a howl of anguish. In the chill Sunday-afternoon stillness it echoed off slate and brick like a tomcat locked in battle. An upstairs window slithered open

107

and a man leaned out.

"What the Hell do you think you're doing, you little blighter!" he snarled. "You've woken half the bloody street! What's your name? I'm coming to see your dad."

"Godfrey Fanshaw," I yelled.

"You're a bloody liar, too. Think I believe that? You wait there!"

I was already running as the window slammed down. He'd never catch me. Not with the start I'd got. Soon all I could hear was the rhythm of my feet on the pavement— Godfrey Fanshaw, Godfrey Fanshaw, Godfrey Fanshaw, Godfrey Fanshaw, Godfrey Fanshaw, Godfrey Fanshaw ...

· Under the Mansions ·

Nobody could explain the Mansions. Did anyone live there? How come it was so big? You'd need Cinemascope to film its ponds and clearings and the narrow lane that in the end came to the house itself. This looked half like a palace and half like a hideout, Teddy said, as if it had been built long ago by a highwayman who'd struck it rich.

Teddy knew the Mansions better than anyone. Once he'd gone right up the steps to the front entrance and standing on tiptoe he'd tried to peer through the shutters. A noise inside had made him run. Probably a rat, he'd suggested later. Maybe a ghost, many kids had thought ...

Another reason for keeping clear of the Mansions was the Keeper. He was said to patrol the grounds carrying a shotgun. Sometimes he had an Alsatian with him. What he was guarding nobody knew, but there were plenty of guesses. Teddy laughed at all of them. Nothing was being guarded, he declared—except the Mansions itself. The Keeper was just there to make sure it stayed private. The other kids, used to Teddy's wild ideas, smiled and nodded and went on guessing. Getting into the Mansions, they knew, was easy enough. Forcing yourself to stay there was the problem—with the Keeper or his dog about to appear at any moment. Not to mention the stories of mantraps in the grass.

Teddy had a hard job persuading Pete and Jimmy to go to the Mansions at all.

"Come on," he said. "Don't be so puny."

"Who's puny?" shrugged Pete. "Not sure I fancy it, that's all."

"Couldn't care less about it," Jimmy agreed. "Plenty of other things we could do."

"Like what?"

"Well ... like—like going down the rec'," said Jimmy.

"Again? We've been there twice this week already," Teddy scoffed.

"Mad Eric might be there."

"So?"

"We could—you know—play tricks on him."

"Oh, very nice. Now you want to spend the afternoon teasing someone who's not even right in the head. Lovely, I must say."

Jimmy blushed.

"You've teased him before," he accused Teddy.

"Sure," said Teddy. "But only when it's just happened. I've never sort of *planned* it."

"We could go swimming," suggested Pete.

"What with? Got any money?"

"No."

"Jimmy?"

"No."

"It's the Mansions, then. Only thing left."

"What about going back to Jimmy's house and playing Monopoly or something? Or with his racetrack?"

"On a day like this?"

With a sweep of his arm Teddy established that indoors was puny compared with outdoors. Still the other two hung back. Teddy stared at them, baffled.

"What's wrong with the Mansions?" he demanded.

How could they say? It was like trying to describe your fear of heights to a steeple-jack. Pete thought of the shadows there and of spooks. Jimmy thought of the Keeper's dog.

"How about it then?" said Teddy.

"Okay," sighed Pete. "Let's go to the Mansions."

"It'll probably be boring," said Jimmy, swallowing hard.

"No it won"t," Teddy insisted. "You'll see."

The Mansions was at the posh end of town where there were no shops, only big houses and golf-courses and tennis-clubs. Teddy led the way. He was so cheerful even Pete and Jimmy began to feel better.

"Kit'll be sorry he missed this," Pete said.

"It's like an adventure," said Jimmy. "Where is Kit?"

"He's gone out with Godfrey Fanshaw and his Dad," said Pete.

"Didn't they take you?" Teddy asked. Pete shook his head.

"Where have they gone?"

"Don't know."

"Didn't you want to go?"

"This'll be much better," said Pete. "Like a adventure."

Teddy looked at him sharply.

"In a way the Mansions is an adventure," he said. "Do you two know about the Secret Cemetery?"

"The what?"

"That's my name for it, anyway. It's nearly as far in as the house. A sort of private graveyard, all overgrown and crumbling. There's a tombstone there for a dog—carved out, just like for a person."

"A dog?" said Jimmy. "Whose dog?"

"Doesn't say. It just says 'In Memory of Regent, a Faithful Hound to the End, 1864'. Must've belonged to someone at the house."

" Might have belonged to the Keeper," said Pete.

"Might have. Wouldn't have thought he was important enough myself. More like the Master's dog. You know—for when he went shooting pheasants and suchlike."

"What breed?" Jimmy asked.

"Doesn't say. Must've been big, though. I mean, you don't call little dogs 'hound' do you. I'll show you when we get there."

"Are we going that far in?" said Jimmy in alarm. "Nearly to the house?"

" If you like," said Teddy. " Do you want to?"

By now the gates were right in front of them. Just inside was where the trees and shadows and Alsatians and mantraps began. You could see no further than the first bend in the lane.

"Why not?" said Pete, faintly.

"Why not?" echoed Jimmy.

Teddy put a finger to his lips and signalled that they were to copy him.

Through the gates, to one side of the entrance, was the Keeper's lodge. Teddy looked it over carefully, his eyes slit like a spy. He eased the iron-work open, sidled through and darted for the first of the trees. From behind this he beckoned the others. As soon as they'd reached him he was off again to the next tree and the next and the next. They had to follow. Dodging from trunk to trunk, they soon lost sight of the entrance. When they got as far as the pond Teddy called a halt.

"It's okay, now," he explained. "We don't have to be so careful. The first bit is the worst. If you're going to be spotted usually it'll be straight away. After that you should be all right so long as you keep clear of the lane and don't start yodelling or something."

"Have you ever been spotted?" Pete asked.

"Once," Teddy answered.

"What did you do?"

"Ran—full pelt."

"Did you get to the gate ahead of him?"

"Didn't run that way. I ran *into* the Mansions."

"In?" gasped Pete.

They stared at Teddy, awe-struck. There were

times when he seemed super-human. Not that he noticed they were impressed. He was too busy grinning at the water and the greenery. The Mansions did something to Teddy. They'd seen it before when he talked about it—as if it were a kingdom he seldom got to visit though he was the King. If only it did the same for them.

"Not exactly a beauty-spot," Pete remarked.

"What?"

"Here. This."

Pete meant the rattle of wind in the reeds and the thick scum on the pond's surface that made you think of bodies nearly dissolved.

"What's wrong with it?" Teddy asked.

Pete and Jimmy gave each other a despairing smile.

"Let's get going," said Teddy. "That graveyard's just over here."

Just over here was through the thick of the wood—a quarter of a mile of stooping and wrenching and untangling and making sure you didn't let go in case the person behind got hit in the face. At every step Pete and Jimmy expected zig-zags of steel to snap shut on them or a sudden wolf-like spring at their throat.

"Okay," Teddy whispered. "We've arrived."

It was just as he'd said. The graveyard seemed to be sinking under the earth. Where the tombstones weren't ivy-covered they were green with moss. Between them the ferns were knee-high. There was a smell of cat.

"Charming," Pete sniffed.

"It's smashing isn't it," said Teddy, his eyes wide.

"Where's that dog memorial thing?" asked Jimmy.

"There," said Teddy. He pointed. The top of the stone was shaped into an animal's head but was so worn away that it might have been a lion or a monkey or an eagle. You could still read the writing though and Teddy had got it exactly right. None of the other graves were as interesting. Just names and dates and what was left of holy words.

"What's that?" Pete exclaimed.

"It's a tree," said Teddy. "Fallen over. Probably struck by lightning."

"Not *that*. I can see that. I meant behind it. A sort of gap."

"A cave," Jimmy suggested.

In a way it was. The opening wasn't large and when they cleared away the weeds and brambles they found concrete slabs on each side with another resting across.

"Never seen it before," Teddy admitted. "Looks like some sort of entrance. Wonder where it goes?"

Jimmy and Pete held their breath. They both knew what was coming next.

"Course, we could always find out," Teddy went on. " I mean, we could always go in a little way. Later we can come back with torches and do it properly. Who knows what we might find!"

"Probably skeletons," said Pete. "It might be a vault. You know, go under the cemetery."

"It slopes the wrong way for that. You can't see it, but we're not far from the house here. I reckon it's a tunnel that leads into the cellars."

"Or the dungeons," said Jimmy.

Teddy shook his head.

"That's only castles. Only castles had dungeons. Don't suppose the Mansions was ever a castle. I'm going to have a look. Anyone coming with me?"

Pete bent to tie up his shoe-lace. Jimmy had something in his eye and was trying to get it out.

"Make your minds up," said Teddy impatiently. "You can wait here if you like."

Which was worse, though, being with Teddy, or being without Teddy?

A gust of wind helped them decide. From treetops to undergrowth everything that wasn't tombstone shivered.

"Just a little way in, then," said Pete, huskily. "Jimmy?"

"Okay," Jimmy croaked.

Teddy gave a whoop of delight and clambered over the tree-trunk.

Once inside the opening even he was cautious at first. The air was dank and after a few feet it thickened into a blackness that somehow kept just ahead of them. They advanced sideways, like crabs, step by step, with their fingertips—as if by accident—brushing each other.

"The tunnel's dipping," hissed Pete.

His voice was quite flat. No echo.

"It's getting wider, too," said Teddy. "And it's curving. Look back."

There was blackness behind them now. Jimmy gave a shriek and turned it hastily into a cough.

"You all right?" Teddy asked.

"Great. Just got a tickle in my throat. The dust I expect."

It was dusty. And slithery underfoot. Pete thought of rats.

"Think this is far enough?" he said hopefully.

"What?"

"Don't want to go in too far, do we?"

"Just a bit further—we could discover something!"

"Like what?"

"Oh, I don't know ... Frankenstein's Monster, maybe."

Teddy said it so matter-of-factly that Pete and Jimmy stopped dead in their tracks. It was this that saved them. They heard Teddy shuffle forward to the brink of whatever was there. They heard him stumble and a frantic scuffling as he fell and went on falling. Then came a distant crack of bone against something harder. After this there was no sound at all.

"Teddy?" whispered Pete. "Teddy? Are you okay?"

Already they knew he wasn't.

"Is he alive?" Jimmy whimpered. "Teddy?"

"He could be knocked out," said Pete.

"But what can we do? We can't even see. We could go over the edge ourselves."

Pete thought about that and licked his lips.

"We'll have to get help. We'll have to fetch someone."

"What, both of us? What about Teddy—suppose he wakes up and he's all on his own? Down there ..."

"One of us'll have to stay."

"Which one?" Jimmy asked.

They stared at the extra darkness that each of them made. They imagined being left there alone. With Teddy.

"You're oldest," Jimmy said.

"All right," replied Pete thickly. "I'll stay. But be as quick as you can. Tell them to get the Fire Brigade and—and an ambulance. Don't waste any time."

"See you then."

"Sprint like mad," Pete begged. "Really fast."

"Goodbye Teddy," Jimmy called.

He was gone before Pete could say any more.

Pete crouched against the side of the tunnel with his knees under his chin, hugging himself. Wherever he looked—up or down or around—he saw a ghost about to appear from the dark. Maybe Teddy's ghost. It was worse when he shut his eyes. Each second he heard a gibber or a cackle or a scream on the point of splitting the silence. Teddy's scream, perhaps. What if he put his fingers in his ears too? He tried—and was terrified of being touched at any moment by something that sneaked up unseen and unheard. Possibly Teddy ... with blood on him and a stump like Thingy's. Could he last until the grown-ups arrived? Could nothing be done till then?

Slowly, tremblingly, Pete shifted his position. He spread himself out in the dust and on his knees and elbows began to crawl towards the pit. That way he couldn't possibly topple over ... could he?

It came sooner than he'd expected: a sudden, rough edge and thin air. Pete peered down. Was it really less dark there or was he just getting used to it? Not that it mattered. He still couldn't see Teddy or anything else. With his fingertips he felt along the brink and almost at once found the ladder. It was iron, and rusty and loose in its fixing. Also it stretched down to Teddy. Or maybe it didn't. Maybe it stopped halfway, however far halfway was. Maybe it would break off altogether and he would land on top of Teddy. Pete cupped his hands to his mouth.

"Teddy! Teddy!" he shouted. "It's Pete! I'm here!"

This time there was a faint echo to his voice. But there was no answer. Pete lay with the ladder in his hands. He could scrape it backwards and forwards in the stonework about half-an-inch. In his mind he pictured the descent—rung by rung, heartbeat by heartbeat—and what he might find if he got to the bottom. Especially he pictured what he might find if he got to the bottom.

Pete sighed and shifted his position again. Uneasily, still shaking, he turned himself round and worked himself backwards until he had a foot on the first of the rungs. With a grip on the ladder so tight that his knuckles hurt he lowered himself over the edge.

Out in the daylight Jimmy ran. His getaway from the graveyard took a jump, a sidestep, and less than a dozen strides. Sheer pace carried him through the worst of the wood.

He skirted the pond flat out and reached the lane breathless and with a stitch in his side. Only as he approached the Keeper's lodge did he slow down. He stopped at the wooden gate, gasping. It was a tall gate and a tall fence for so small a front garden. No dog could leap over it—not even the Alsatian that lay stretched across the path.

At first Jimmy thought he hadn't woken it. Then it pricked its ears, and lifted its head. A growl muttered at the back of its throat.

"Good boy," Jimmy quavered.

The Alsatian bristled and snarled and stood up. Its snout wrinkled, baring its teeth. Jimmy snatched his hand from the gate.

"Hey mister!" he called. "Mister!"

There was no response except from the dog. It all but spat with fury. The noise in its throat was far worse than a bark. Was this part of their killer-training? With a howl like a wolf afterwards?

"Hey! Hey! Mr Keeper! Are you there?"

Jimmy's shout sounded feeble even to him. No one inside would hear it. And no one would come to rescue Teddy.

"Help! We need help—please! Help, mister! Please!"

The door stayed closed. No face appeared at the window. Even the dog's fuss got no worse. Should he take the risk? Jimmy lifted the latch and pushed the gate open. Just in time he slammed it shut again with only the paling between him and the snap of the Alsatian's jaws.

What could he do now? Try another house?

The nearest was half-a-mile away. Besides, the Keeper was at home. Somehow Jimmy knew that. The problem was how to attract his attention from outside the fence.

When the answer came to him Jimmy acted at once before he lost his nerve. He found a heavy stone, thought of Teddy, and flung it as hard as he could at the window. It shattered in a jangle of glass so loud any kid in the world would have run. Not Jimmy. Almost sick with terror he stayed. It seemed to him that the door burst open in slow motion and the Keeper's roar of anger lasted forever. But when he saw Jimmy his rage faded.

"Please, please mister," Jimmy babbled, "Teddy's fallen down a hole or a crevasse or something in that tunnel by the cemetery and he's dead maybe and I'm sorry about the window but I was scared of the dog but please mister Pete said get a fire engine and an ambulance and run like mad in case he's only knocked out" Jimmy burst into tears.

After this it was adults only. The nine-nine-nine call and the arrival of police car, ambulance and fire engine with ropes and flashlights and res-cue-gear seemed nothing to do with Jimmy. Or with Pete, who was found in the meat-pit cuddling the injured party. This was what they called Teddy—the injured party. Somehow it left him out too.

"... A sort of olden days icebox," Pete explained later. "That was what it was. Where carcasses and Poultry and stuff was stored. Course it hasn't been used for years. Except by Teddy. Nearly stored his carcass."

"Shut up," said Jimmy.

It was all over now but the thought of it still made him shiver.

"When does he come out of hospital?" he asked.

"About a week, they reckon, because of concussion or something. But his leg'll be in plaster for about six weeks."

"That's till the end of the holidays."

"More than that. We'll be back at school. Teddy won't be roaming round the Mansions much this summer."

"Neither will we," said Jimmy. "Will we?"

For some while they both considered it.

"Don't suppose we'll get time," Pete said at last. "Not with the money Teddy's Mum gave us. We'll be too busy swimming or going to the pictures. We can even afford to take people with us."

"She even said she'd pay for the broken window. And she didn't tell us off. She said we were *brave*."

"That's what she said," agreed Pete.

"Were you brave?" Jimmy asked. "I was frightened stiff."

"I was frightened stiff, too."

They grinned at each other sheepishly then, for the tenth time, got out the money and counted it.

"We may be a couple of scaredycats but at least we're rich scaredycats," Pete remarked.

"That's true. But I'd rather be a daredevil like Teddy."

"So would I," sighed Pete.

Yet in a funny way they both knew what Teddy's Mum meant.

Where it Stops, Nobody Knows
by Amy Ehrlich
£2.99

When Nina and her mother settle in Vermont, Nina thinks it's a perfect place to live. So why does her mother insist that they move again? Nina begins to realise the frightening truth – they are not moving in search of something, they are running away.

Nobody's Family is Going to Change
by Louise Fitzhugh
£2.99

Emma Sheridan is an intelligent black 11-year-old, a compulsive eater, and wants to be a distinguished lawyer, like her father. But her parents see marriage as the goal for Emma, and, in her rebellion against parental prejudices, Emma learns much about herself and others.

In a Place of Danger by Paula Fox
£2.99

Emma was scared when she went to stay with Aunt Bea. Scared for her ill father, and scared of her aunt who didn't seem to be normal. But as the weeks go by and Emma meets a new friend, she realises why Aunt Bea is so strange and why nothing is ever what it seems.

Into the Dark by Nicholas Wilde
£2.99

Because Matthew is blind, he has hardly ever been anywhere without his mother. Until, on a week's holiday in Norfolk, he makes friends with Roly, who takes him to the marshes. Here he finds a new world, but a mysterious one, in which he discovers a strange and fearful secret about his new friend.

Shiva by J. H. Brennan
£2.50

A potent tale of adventure and emotion set during the Ice Age. Tribal legends become frighteningly real when 12-year-old Shiva comes face to face with a young ogre – a creature of folklore.

The Crone by J. H. Brennan
£2.75

When Shiva, a young orphan girl, is captured by the fearsome Barradik tribe and accused of the Hag's murder, it seems that her fate is sealed. But everyone, especially her captors, have forgotten her friendship with the formidable ogres. *The Crone* continues the story begun in *Shiva*...

The Silver Crown by Robert O'Brien
£3.50

Ellen had known all along she was a queen, and the silver crown she found on her pillow only went to prove it. Proudly wearing her new present, she tiptoed out for an early morning walk that was to lead her into the realms of deepest danger. Was it the crown they were after – or her?

The Phantom Tollbooth by Norton Juster
£3.50

Miserable Milo flopped down in his chair and caught sight of the giant package. "One genuine turnpike tollbooth" reads the note attached, and, for want of something better to do, Milo jumps into the car and journeys through a land in which words and numbers rudely defy the dictates of order and sense.

Edith Herself by Ellen Howard
£2.50

It was after Edith went to live with her sister Alena and her family that she started to have epileptic fits, but she's determined to lead a normal life in spite of them. This is the story of how she faced up to the problem, found friends, and a place for herself in Alena's family.

A Sound of Chariots by Mollie Hunter
£2.50

From her earliest recollection Bridie McShane and her father had shared a very special understanding. Tough yet acutely sensitive, she has inherited his fighting spirit, his dauntless honesty and his deep love of booksand words. Desolated by his death, she learns to make him live again through her writing.

When Hitler Stole Pink Rabbit
by Judith Kerr
£2.99

When nine-year-old Anna and her family success-fully escape from Nazi Germany, the hardships of refugee life begin. From Switzerland to Paris to London, Anna and her brother Max learn English, French and How to Survive Life.

A Free Man on Sunday by Fay Sampson
£2.50

Edie's father and his rambling friends, banned from walking in the countryside they love, plan a mass trespass on one of highest peaks. For once Edie is not allowed to go with them. Secretly she does so, causing more trouble than she would have believed possible.

Instant Sisters by Rose Impey
£2.99

It's an instant recipe for disaster when two feuding teenagers from different parents share a tiny bedroom because one girl's father has moved in with the other girl's mother.

A Friend Like Phoebe by Marilyn Kaye
£2.50

Phoebe was trying not to be jealous. And she wasn't, not really. At least, she didn't particularly want to be doing what her sisters were doing. But she didn't want to be left out, either. And if her sisters were going to be famous, she had to be famous too. The question was, how?

Private, Keep Out by Gwen Grant
£2.50

"I have written a book. It's all about the street we live on – me and our Mam and Dad, and our Peter and Tone, and Lucy, Rose and Joe. They're my brothers and sisters, worst luck." A highly amusing story, about growing up just after the War.

One Way Only by Gwen Grant
£1.95

Home safe and well after going to school in Kent, the lively, lovable Nottinghamshire lass finds her brothers and sisters as aggravating as before, "stuck in my life like trip-up wires and I keep falling over them".

Wagstaffe the Wind-Up Boy by Jan Needle
£2.50

Wagstaffe is so awful that his mother and father run away from home. Wagstaffe celebrates by playing a practical joke on a lorry on the M62 – a stupid thing to do: he's squashed flat. A brilliant doctor patches him up so he can undertake some great adventures.

Dakota of the White Flats by Philip Ridley
£2.75

Is there a monster hidden in old Medusa's carefully guarded supermarket trolley? Ten-year-old Dakota Pink cannot resist having a look, and before she knows it she is sailing towards an impenetrable fortress along a river full of killer eels.

Mercedes Ice by Philip Ridley
£1.95

In Shadow Point, a menacing and crumbling tower block, Hickory plays at being Queen of the basement with a cloak of cobweb. Her friend Mercedes is a prince, but he longs for his kingdom to be more colourful.

The Sword in the Stone by T. H. White
£3.99

The story of the enchanted (and enchanting) lessons which the boy nicknamed The Wart learns through his tutor, Merlyn the magician. This richly comic fantasy of King Arthur's times will appeal to all readers.

The Man with Eyes Like Windows
by Gareth Owen
£2.25

Louie's dad is a drifter, for ever pushing off to look for fame and fortune. Eventually his long-suffering wife refuses to have him back, and Louie sets off to find him. His search leads him through adventures, funny and touching, before he finds his father and persuades him to come home.

The Fib by George Layton
£2.99

"I was sick of Gordon Barraclough going on about my old football gear. So I told him it had belonged to my uncle, Bobby Charlton! That was the fib. Then a few days later, we met Bobby Charlton..." Eight short, funny stories about many important issues of adolescent life – school, girlfriends, football, and the problems of keeping in with your mates and getting round Mum.

My Mate Shofiq by Jan Needle
£2.99

When Bernard witnesses the quiet Pakistani boy, Shofiq, defending some younger curry kids against a bully and his gang, he is gradually drawn into friendship with him and discovers they share the same problems at home too. The violent clash between Bernard's gang and the bullies, and the break-up of Shofiq's family under pressure from the authorities, lead to a dramatic and thought-provoking climax.